# Secret Baby for a Damaged Billionaire

LILY CROSS

Copyright © 2023 by Lily Cross.

All rights reserved.

No part of this publication may be reproduced, distributed, or transmitted in any form or by any means, including photocopying, recording, or other electronic or mechanical methods, without the prior written permission of the publisher, except as permitted by U.S. copyright law. For permission requests, contact [include publisher/author contact info].

The story, all names, characters, and incidents portrayed in this production are fictitious. No identification with actual persons (living or deceased), places, buildings, and products is intended or should be inferred.

# Contents

| | |
|---|---:|
| Chapter One (Emily) | 1 |
| Chapter Two (Lucas) | 16 |
| Chapter Three (Emily) | 29 |
| Chapter Four (Lucas) | 40 |
| Chapter Five (Emily) | 49 |
| Chapter Six (Lucas) | 62 |
| Chapter Seven (Emily) | 71 |
| Chapter Eight (Lucas) | 80 |
| Chapter Nine (Emily) | 89 |
| Chapter Ten (Lucas) | 99 |
| Chapter Eleven (Emily) | 113 |
| Chapter Twelve (Lucas) | 124 |
| Chapter Thirteen (Emily) | 132 |
| Chapter Fourteen (Lucas) | 143 |

| | |
|---|---:|
| Chapter Fifteen (Emily) | 152 |
| Chapter Sixteen (Lucas) | 166 |
| Chapter Seventeen (Emily) | 178 |
| Chapter Eighteen (Lucas) | 190 |
| Chapter Nineteen (Emily) | 202 |
| Chapter Twenty (Lucas) | 213 |
| Chapter Twenty-One (Emily) | 223 |
| Chapter Twenty-Two (Lucas) | 235 |
| Chapter Twenty-Three (Emily) | 244 |
| Chapter Twenty-Four (Lucas) | 253 |
| Chapter Twenty-Five (Emily) | 264 |
| Special Offer | 274 |

# Chapter One (Emily)

Stepping into the grand ballroom, my stilettos click sharply on the marble floor, and I feel all eyes on me as if my single status is in direct disrespect to my best friend's engagement party. The chandeliers cast a mocking golden glow. A wave of insecurity washes over me as I search for my seat among the round tables, ivory linens, and centerpieces bursting with pink peonies.

I spot Chloe in a cloud of tulle, her Oscar de la Renta dress exuding classic glamor as she stands near the champagne tower, her cheeks flushed with excitement. She waves me over enthusiastically, nearly upending a glass of bubbly in the process.

"Emily! You made it!" She throws her arms around me, the familiar scent of her perfume instantly easing my discomfort. I relax in her embrace, giddy energy radiating off of her.

"You look beautiful," I say. "I can't believe this is actually happening."

"I know," she gushes. "I feel like we've been planning our weddings since college." She catches herself and bares her teeth apologetically.

Her soon-to-be mother-in-law appears and takes hold of her arm. "Chloe, come see my cousins from Ohio. They're dying to meet you."

Chloe rolls her eyes and shakes her head as she's whisked away.

I scan the tables again, searching for my seat, trying to forget about the memory of us planning our weddings together, destination Cape Cod, and starting our married lives in the same neighborhood in the posh suburbs of Boston. But then Dominic dumps me out of the blue, shattering those plans to bits, returning me to square one, while Chloe forges ahead.

"Emily, over here." My attention is pulled to a table in the middle of the room. Chloe's fashion-industry work friends call me over, pointing to an empty seat.

"You look stunning!" one of them gushes, her designer dress putting my little black number to shame. She touches my arm, her red nails a jarring contrast against my sun-starved skin. "How do you get your hair that perfect strawberry blonde color?"

The others chime in, showering me with compliments on my makeup, wondering if I go to the gym every day, and asking how I could possibly be single. Their kind remarks accentuate my awkward dateless state, so I force a smile, taking a large swallow of champagne to avoid responding. I know the reply of being cheated on and my hair color being natural would only bore them.

Twenty-five. The number looms in my mind as the conversation drifts to wedding details and future family plans. In a few short months, I'll reach that milestone, with nothing to show for it but a neglected dating life and an overscheduled calendar of contract negotiations and volunteering at the dog shelter.

The music shifts to something loud and pounding, the bass vibrating through my chest. Couples flood the dance floor, spinning and twirling under the swirling lights.

I stand abruptly, nearly upending my glass. "I'll be right back."

The girls barely notice my exit, already deep in debate over the pros and cons of local or destination weddings. I weave through the crowd, dodging Chloe's doting aunts who always ask me when I'm going to get married, practically squeezing my cheeks every time. The heat and noise and laughter press in on me until I think I might suffocate.

The lobby is blissfully empty, silent but for the muted music from the ballroom. Taking a deep inhale, and closing my eyes, I kick off my heels and drop onto an upholstered loveseat, just as someone else lands on the sofa with me at the same time.

The couch shifts from the sudden weight and hits the wall with a thud. I turn in shock and my eyes meet a piercing blue gaze beneath knitted brows. I flush, taking in the sight of a ruggedly handsome man, sitting only inches from me, dressed in a sharp charcoal designer suit, with muscular broad shoulders and a sharp jawline.

He tips his head, cropped hair giving a strong, military vibe. "Not a fan of the swan napkins?"

His joke catches me off guard and puts me immediately at ease.

"More like all the crazy aunts asking when my turn to get married will be," I scoff.

"No surprise. My aunts have been doing that to everyone all night, including me." He shakes his head, sitting deeper on the couch.

"I—what? *Your* aunts?" My eyes widen from what must be the earliest I've ever put my foot in my mouth, but also from the curiosity of how he might be connected to Chloe's aunts.

He groans lightly, pinching the bridge of his nose. "Gets to be a bit much, doesn't it?"

I grin. "So, I take it you're not much for big family parties either." I glance at the couch and then back toward the ballroom, making it clear that we're both avoiding it.

He presses his lips together. "Noise and chaos send me running for the hills." I catch his eyes moving over my dress as he casually looks in the direction of the music. "I'm Lucas, by the way." He holds out a hand, gazing straight into my soul.

"Emily." I take his hand, startled by the warmth and strength of his grip. I hope he can't sense my nerves, but he's just so hot.

His eyes light up with understanding as a grin spreads across his inviting lips. "Ah. So, you're the infamous Emily."

My spine straightens, as I wonder who this gorgeous man is, and how he knows about me. With my brow furrowed, I ask, "Infamous?"

And just as the pieces start coming together in my mind, he confirms my suspicion.

"According to my sister, you're the bad influence. The one who suggests skydiving or crowd surfing as intriguing afternoon activities." He glances at me, brows lifted.

I grin under his close scrutiny, his blue eyes piercing into mine. "You're Chloe's brother?" I ask, ignoring his accusation. "The one who's been away for like, a decade?" I pull my gaze away from him, struggling to not stare at his chiseled jaw and broad chest. How could Chloe not have mentioned how gorgeous her older brother was?

"Avoiding the point in question?" he teases. "So, you admit you're a bad influence?" His eyes move over me like a warm blanket, heating me up inside.

"Chloe and I are a good match," I say with a defensive tone. "We balance each other out. She's usually the crazy one, and I'm the rational one." I stare at him, wondering what he's heard.

"Hmm, not exactly how I heard it, but, either way, it's meant as a compliment," he says, holding up his hands in a peaceful gesture. "It just seems like any reckless adventure Chloe embarks on; your name always seems to be attached."

"Yeah, well, she *is* my best friend." I lift one shoulder, then study him more closely. "She talks about you a lot," I say. "You were in the military. For a long time. She missed you."

He nods. "Afghanistan." And then falls silent, looking away.

I swallow hard, remembering Chloe telling me stories of missions that went bad for him, his patrols being ambushed, land mines and explosions, losing members of his platoon, his friends. I study him for a moment, taking in the creases fanning out from the corners of his eyes, premature lines that revealed his difficult experiences.

"Well, she's glad to have you back," I say, knowing how much he means to her from the endless stories. "Weren't you in Dubai for a while?" I remember Chloe mentioning him making a fortune there.

He turns his attention back to me as he clears the lost gaze in his expression. "I stopped there for a while, on my way back home."

Our eyes meet again, and this time I don't look away.

"So, what do you do?" he asks, moving the attention off of himself. "Same as Chloe? Fashion design and social media shit?"

His low-interest tone annoys me. Chloe has an amazing career, one she built from the ground up. Her eye for fashion is impeccable and she'd branded herself as an iconic influencer, sharing trends and marketing for designer labels.

"I wish," I say, narrowing my eyes. "Chloe's success is insane." I have to get that jab in there. "But no, I'm a freelance contract negotiator." I shrug. "Kind of a badass when it comes to hashing out business deals."

"Oh, you're a badass now?" he says, grinning. "I knew it. Well, hopefully, you still save a little of your time to have some fun." He gazes at me with a sultry smile.

I'm not sure how I feel about him yet, whether he's a complete asshole, or maybe just a tough exterior, protecting whatever wounds he has inside. It's difficult to decide, but the obvious fact is the one that tingles between my legs. He's gorgeous, strong, and masculine beyond belief. I imagine he'd be amazing in bed and think of him taking me over, devouring me.

As a blush rises to my cheeks from my spicy thoughts, a voice shoots out from behind me, bringing me back to the present moment.

"Emily! I was looking for you," Chloe gushes, hobbling over to us with heels that are too high, likely causing blisters. She plops down in the chair across from us, oblivious to the tension hanging thick in the air. "I've been looking for both of you, actually. The toasts are about to start."

I blink, shaken by the spell Lucas had cast over me. "On our way," I say with a forced smile.

Chloe looks at both of us as her eyes reveal her surprise. "So, you guys met each other," she sings. "I was planning on introducing you." She turns her attention to Lucas. "I told you she was awesome. You have to consider her for your business. Trust me, I know what I'm talking about."

I stare at Chloe, having no idea what she is talking about. Sure, I am in a drought for clients at the moment, but I wasn't about to disclose that to *him*. And working for her brother was not something I'd ever considered. My mind is currently elsewhere when it came to what I wanted to do with Lucas.

Chloe beams and rushes off to corral the rest of the guests. Lucas stands and holds out a hand to help me up. I quickly wiggle my feet into my heels.

"Shall we?" he asks softly.

Heart pounding, I place my hand in his and rise to my feet. His grip lingers for a second too long, and I find myself hoping the night won't end with the reception.

"We shall," I say, pulse racing at the promise in his smile.

#

We rejoin the party, acutely aware of each other in a way that makes the noisy ballroom fade into the background. Lucas guides me toward the bar area with a high table near the front. As the toasts begin, he pulls out my chair and I sit, happy to be away from the crowded tables.

Throughout the speeches, I feel the heat of his gaze on the side of my face, wordless but intense. As Chloe and her new fiancé, Scott, share their first dance, Lucas reaches for my hand on the table and casually taps his fingers across my knuckles. A sizzle runs up my arm, causing my air to suck in.

"We should go somewhere quieter," he says. "I'd love to talk more, get to know you better." His burning gaze leaves me little choice.

It's very unlike me to take a man up on such an offer, but he was Chloe's brother, so it's not like he's a stranger. And Chloe seemed genuinely happy that we had found each other at her party, her approval clear. And, I have to admit, the loud music and overwhelming crowd are too much for me. Judging by the strain on his face, it seems like it's too much for him too.

"Sure," I say. "What did you have in mind?"

"A drink. Softer music," he states, keeping his eyes fixed on mine.

"Okay," I agree. "Somewhere less... well, just less."

He nods, taking my hand in his. He leads me out of the loud ballroom back into the hotel foyer, and we both let out huge exhales, leaving the chaos of the party behind us.

"What did Chloe mean about you needing help with your business?" I ask, thinking about her unexpected suggestion to have me work for him and wondering how on earth I could be of use to him. "What kind of work do you do now?"

He walks me across the bright lobby area, toward the small bar near the front entrance. A few hotel guests sit on high stools, sipping their dark liquors, likely preparing for their next business meetings the following day. Instead of seeking a table, Lucas walks up to the shiny mahogany counter, gesturing to the barman.

They have a brief exchange, and then Lucas turns back to me.

"MMA," he says in a flat tone. "BJJ."

"What?" I look at him, furrowing my brow.

"Mixed martial arts," he states, tipping his head slightly. "Brazilian Jujitsu."

I stare at him in confusion as if he's speaking another language.

He smirks. "I have a chain of sparring gyms, dojos if you will. Top-ranking fighters on my roster, known globally. I'm looking to expand to Dubai." He reaches for the champagne bottle and glasses that the barman hands him. "Thanks, man." And he lifts his eyebrows flirtatiously. "Shall we?"

He heads over to the elevators, pressing the call button, as I follow in curiosity. We wait in silence, anticipation thrumming between us. The doors slide open, and we step inside, Lucas immediately presses the button for the top floor.

"You have a room here?" I ask, eyes widening.

"Mm-hmm." He holds my gaze in a dramatic pause, waiting as the elevator climbs.

My mind races, imagining being alone with him, having the privacy to do what I want to him. The thrill excites every nerve in my body as I anticipate letting my guard down and throwing all rules of dating etiquette out the window. I want to be alone with Lucas, and he clearly has the same idea for me.

As the elevator climbs higher, he turns his body toward mine, spreading his stance wide as he closes in on me. I back against the wall, unable to avoid his intense posture and my breath quickens. He holds his hands out on either side of me, one holding the champagne bottle and the other with the glasses.

He moves his face close to mine. "Are you comfortable coming up to my suite with me?" he whispers, his breath tickling my lips. "The views are spectacular."

The elevator chimes and stops its ascent, and I nod. "Yes," I say. "I'd love to see it." *Though the views are the last thing I care about seeing*, feeling the heat that radiated through his perfectly fitted designer suit.

I can hardly believe my own illicit thoughts. I had convinced myself that my desire to be with a man had dried up after Dominic blindsided me, sleeping with his side piece in our own bed. But now, Lucas woke something inside me, something ravenous, and I feel alive again.

The elevator doors slide open and Lucas gestures for me to follow him as he steps out, leading me down the hall to his suite. I hold the glasses for him as he fumbles with the keycard, swearing under his breath, and I can't help but laugh at his eagerness.

As soon as he gets the doors open, he invites me in, switching on the lights and kicking the door shut. As I marvel at the enormous, elegant space, the amazing sky view out the floor-to-ceiling windows displaying all of Boston, he takes the glasses from my hands and places them on the side table with the bottle of champagne. And without a word, he pins me against the wall, pressing his muscular frame on my body, allowing me to feel his strength and his power.

He lifts his hands, framing my face, and whispers, "I'm sorry, I want to kiss you so badly."

He locks my eyes with his, waiting for my permission, and every muscle in my body melts from the desperation in his gaze. And with the same level of desire rising within me, I tilt my face toward his, inviting him in.

With a slight grin, he lowers his mouth to mine, hesitating a tiny distance from my lips, making me grow hungrier. And then he kisses me, strong and urgent, causing every nerve in my body to explode. It feels like weeks and months of pent-up longing between the two of us, unleashed in a single moment of connection. And I melt into him, fingers running through his short hair and around his neck.

He breaks away for a moment, gasping. "Jesus," he breathes heavily, eyes trailing along my body. "What is it about you? You're driving me wild," he growls, trailing hot, open-mouthed kisses down along my throat. I gasp, tilting my head to give him better access. "You have no idea how long it's been for me."

His voice is low and vulnerable, making me want him even more, as he buries his face in my hair, inhaling me.

"I want you, Lucas," I gasp, desire burning white-hot in my veins, trailing my hands down his chest, feeling the contours of his muscles through his shirt.

Without another word, he scoops me into his arms, carrying me into the bedroom. We tumble onto the mattress together, and he kneels over me, unbuttoning his shirt without taking his eyes off of me. As he throws his shirt to the floor, the sight of his bare chest makes me weak, all thoughts of any consequence flee my mind, replaced only by a singular need to be as close to him as humanly possible.

As my gaze trails down his stomach, landing on his belt, he grins, reaching around my back, and pulling on the zipper of my dress. In seconds, our clothes are on the floor, and he props his weight over me, kissing me with hot desire.

Our bodies tangle together, enjoying every touch and every caress, as I allow myself to surrender, becoming lost in him, setting my heart on a collision course with destiny.

# Chapter Two (Lucas)

The scent of Emily's perfume lingers on my skin, a haunting reminder of the intimacy we shared. I close my eyes and inhale deeply, transported back to the feel of her soft body pressed against mine. She slipped out of my hotel suite earlier, gathered her things, leaving a sweet kiss on my lips that only taunts me now. The memory elicits an unwelcome ache in my chest.

Damn it. I can't afford to feel this way about her. Or any woman.

With a frustrated sigh, I roll out of bed and drag myself into the bathroom. The cold tile floor offers a sharp contrast to the warmth of the bed, a welcome distraction as I turn on the shower and step under the spray.

The water washes away the evidence of our night together, but it does nothing to ease the turmoil in my mind. I shouldn't have given in to the attraction between us. I knew better. But when she looked up at me with those bright green eyes and pouty lips, her curves tempting every part of me, all rational thought left. I was powerless to resist her pull.

Now I have to face the consequences. I'll see her again today, Chloe already made the arrangement through text, and there's no avoiding the tension that's sure to hang thick in the air between Emily and me. The memory of her soft moans and the feel of her nails digging into my back will make it impossible to treat her as just a business associate.

How did I let this happen? I swore off relationships after my last tour of duty. My heart has already been ripped out enough times. The darkness that lives inside me is too dangerous now to expose to anyone. But one night with Emily, and all those walls came crumbling down, leaving me exposed.

The water begins to run cold, dragging me from my brooding thoughts. I turn off the faucet and step out of the shower, grabbing a towel to dry off. There's no going back now. I'll have to find a way to compartmentalize, bury my feelings when we're together, and avoid acting on the attraction that simmers just below the surface.

It's the only way I can keep her safe. And me. Even if it means denying myself the one thing I crave most. Her.

#

As I walk into the gym, my black belts and trophies line the entryway, while the grunts of grappling fighters fill the air. This is my world now—far from my days as a Navy SEAL, but still closely tied to the discipline and strength that defined my time in the military. As the owner of this world-renowned jujitsu training enterprise, I keep focused on expanding beyond Boston and adding additional prized fighters to my roster. I just need some help with closing the deals that will launch my business to the next level, straight out of Southie to the top of the global spotlight.

"Lucas!" Chloe's voice breaks through the noise, and I turn to see her waving at me with Emily by her side. Emily looks like a breath of fresh air, stopping my heart momentarily, her floral dress cascading over her alluring body, her long blonde hair tied back with loose stands teasing her shoulders. Flashes of our incredible night together pass through my mind, creating a renewed desire to have her beneath me again. But I quickly shift my feelings to the professional realm, suppressing any frivolous emotions that could derail me.

"Hey, Chloe," I greet, trying to keep my gaze steady and my voice casual despite the effect Emily has on me. "Good to see you again, Emily." I nod my head in greeting.

"Figured I'd introduce you two properly," Chloe says with a grin, nudging Emily forward, clueless about how much we got to know each other the night before. "I'm so glad you two had a chance to break the ice at the engagement party."

Emily shoots Chloe a playful glare before turning to me with a smile that makes my heart race. "Nice to see you again too, Lucas," she says with a subtle smirk.

"Lucas," Chloe interjects, pulling my attention back to her, "I wanted you guys to have a chance to talk business. I really think Emily would be perfect to help you with your expansion. She's an amazing contract negotiator and could bring in the top talent you need."

"Is that so?" I ask, trying to hide the skepticism in my voice. I can't deny my attraction to Emily, but I also can't imagine this delicate, sensual woman going head-to-head with hardened fighters and their managers.

"Trust me, Lucas," Chloe insists. "She's more than capable."

"Chloe's right," Emily chimes in, her eyes meeting mine with a confidence that surprises and intrigues me. "I'm good at what I do, and I think I could really help you out." Her eyes narrow slightly, noticing my distance.

As much as I want to believe her, I can't shake the feeling that mixing business with pleasure might end badly for both of us. I allow my wall to climb higher, knowing my PTSD from my military days is easily triggered, awakening a fight response I can't always control, and I need to be careful about who I let into my life.

"Please, Lucas," Chloe begs. "You have to let go a little, allow someone to help you out. You can't always do it alone." She glares at me, knowing how stubborn I am, and keenly aware of my trauma damage. But she's right. If I want my enterprise to go to the top globally, with my fighters winning world championships, I need expert help that I can trust.

I trust Chloe's professional recommendation and it would save me time from interviewing others. "We can discuss details," I finally agree, still hesitant but willing to give Emily a chance, "to see if you're a good fit."

"Sure." Emily nods, her eyes grow vacant as she feels my cold gaze. Beneath her agreement to further our discussions, I see she's hurt by my doubt and distance. Despite the affection we shared, I have to box it away as a one-night stand, determined to keep things professional between us at this point. And if that means treating her skeptically and blandly, then that's how it has to be.

Chloe grabs hold of Emily's arm and does a small dance. Their close, playful relationship is evident, and I can't help but feel a twinge of envy. "This is going to be so perfect," she gushes.

"Come on, Em," she encourages her, giving her a squeeze. "Tell him about that time you negotiated that massive deal for the whiskey company. Isn't it owned by that Irish MMA fighter, you know, the one with the green yacht and the gorilla tattoo?"

My eyes widen. "You mean...?" I stare at Chloe, understanding now why she thought the collaboration could be a good one between Emily and me.

"Yup," she says, not even allowing me to finish my sentence.

"Chloe, I got it from here," Emily says, casting a nervous glance in my direction.

"I know. I know," she says, ignoring Emily's humble approach. "She's exactly what you need, Lucas," she continues. "And, Emily, you could use the distraction after Dom's bullshit."

"Chloe!" Emily barks, embarrassment written all over her face.

"Sorry," Chloe murmurs sheepishly, finally releasing Emily from her embrace. "But it's true. You deserve better, you need to move on, and this job is perfect for you."

I throw my hands up. "Okay. We're done here." I turn my attention to my fighters on the mat, the smell of their sweat and aggression filling the space. "I'll book a meeting for us to go over details," I say, trying not to let my resolve waver. She may be beautiful and passionate, but I need someone who can deliver results for my gym. And I have to keep reminding myself—business first.

\#

I weigh my options, considering the pros and cons of hiring Emily. Sure, she's got an impressive resume and Chloe vouches for her, but can I really trust her to handle the high-pressure world of contract negotiations for my prized fighters? After all, our intimate night together gave me the impression that she was more delicate than tough, a gorgeous sexual being rather than a cutthroat deal closer. And honestly, she seemed too nice, soft. I could see rivals walking all over her.

Chloe's words replay in my mind, snapping me out of my thoughts. *"I know you're hesitant, but Emily is really good at her job. She has a knack for getting the best deals,"* she had said. So, I relent, exhaling deeply. I make the final decision to give her a shot, to prove herself.

Emily joins me the next day at the gym for our meeting, dressed professionally in a tailored suit, her expression serious and determined. I appreciate the contrast between this side of her and the passionate woman I shared a bed with. But as much as those memories tempt me, I have to maintain a professional distance. I need Emily focused on her job, not on reigniting our chemistry.

"Morning, Emily," I greet, keeping my voice neutral.

"Good morning, Lucas," she replies, barely meeting my eyes before turning her attention to a stack of documents on the table. I can sense the tension between us, but I stubbornly refuse to acknowledge it.

"Let's get started, then," I say, taking a seat across from her. "We've got a potential deal with a rising star in MMA, his jujitsu is world-class, and I want to make sure we're getting the best terms possible. I'd like to get your take on it, to see if this is something you can handle."

She glances at me with a hint of annoyance behind her gaze. "Of course," she agrees, her tone equally bland as she flips through the contract, making notes and asking relevant questions. I watch her work, impressed by her focus and attention to detail. Maybe she does have what it takes to succeed in this business.

"I've found a few clauses that could be negotiated in your favor," she suggests after some time, and I nod to her to continue.

As she expertly outlines her strategy for securing a better deal, I feel a grudging respect for her abilities. Maybe Chloe was right—perhaps Emily is more than just a pretty face and a fun night between the sheets. But as we continue to work together, I can't shake the nagging doubt that lingers at the back of my mind.

"Great work, Emily," I say when we wrap up our meeting, carefully maintaining a polite distance despite the lingering tension between us. "Can you come back tomorrow to take action on this?"

"Yes," she replies, giving me a small smile before gathering her things. "See you then."

As I watch her walk away, I can't deny that I'm attracted to her in more ways than one. But for now, I need to keep my focus on the success of my gym, and that means keeping my eyes off her incredible ass.

\#

The following day, I watch Emily from across the gym as she talks on the phone with a potential fighter's agent. Her brow furrows slightly, and she tucks a strand of hair behind her ear in frustration. She's trying to hide it, but I can tell the call isn't going well.

When she hangs up with a sigh, I approach her. "Trouble in paradise?"

She shoots me a glare. "Nothing I can't handle. This fighter's manager is being unreasonable, but I have a few tricks up my sleeve."

I raise an eyebrow, surprised by her confidence. "Do you now?"

"Yes, as a matter of fact." She straightens, staring me down defiantly. "I may not have years of experience in this industry, but I know how to get what I want. And your gym is going to benefit from it."

A smile tugs at the corner of my lips as I fold my arms across my chest. "Prove it."

Emily smirks, grabbing the phone and dialing the fighter's manager again. I listen in disbelief as she lays out an airtight counteroffer, backed by facts and figures to support her case. By the end of the call, the manager has not only agreed to her terms but also thanked her for the "opportunity."

When Emily hangs up again, her eyes meet mine in challenge. But this time, all I see is her skill, her passion for the job, and her dedication to the success of my gym. She has proven herself in more ways than one, and for the first time, I realize Chloe was right all along.

Emily is perfect for this job.

"Well?" she prompts, hands on her hips.

I clear my throat, trying to find the right words. "Call me impressed," I say at last.

Emily's features soften into a smile, her eyes glowing. And in that moment, I know I'm in trouble.

As the day moves on, I bring my focus back to my fighters and my own training, while Emily continues working on the contracts. Grappling in the ring, I exert a massive amount of energy, winning each round, clearing the adrenaline from my veins.

As business operations begin winding down for the day, I check in with Emily to review her progress. As she flips through her notes, I lean over her shoulder for a better look, inhaling the alluring scent of her hair. And just as my thoughts are about to betray me, Chloe bursts through the gym doors, and sees Emily and me in my office going over the revised contracts, and a knowing smile spreads across her face.

"I knew it," she says. "I'm so glad to see you two working so well together." Her tone was deceptively casual, causing me to take a second look. "Lucas, do you have a minute? I wanted to talk to you about something."

Emily excuses herself to make some calls, leaving me alone with my sister. As soon as Emily's out of earshot, Chloe turns to me with a stern look, her dark hair shadowing her features to near sinister levels.

"I saw the way you were looking at her," she says with a sharp look in her eyes. "Don't even think about it, Lucas. I know how much the gym means to you, and I don't want you screwing that up over some crush. I know she's hot, but getting involved with her is not a good idea."

"What are you talking about?" I protest, but I feel the flush creeping up my neck. Chloe knows me too well. "I'm impressed with her skill, nothing more."

"I'm serious," she insists. "Emily is my best friend, and I care about you both too much to see this end in disaster. Keep things professional, or I'll have to find you a new contract negotiator. Got it?"

I open my mouth to argue, but Chloe silences me with a glare. As much as I hate to admit it, she has a point. My life is finally getting back on track after years of struggle, and I can't afford to complicate that now—no matter how intriguing Emily might be.

With a sigh, I nod in resignation. "Message received," I tell Chloe. "Strictly professional."

"Good. I'm glad we understand each other." Chloe smiles, relieved, and gives me a quick hug. "Now, tell me how she's doing. I knew she'd be great."

As we discuss the gym, I glance over at Emily now and then, her laughter drifting over to where we stand. Chloe is right that I need to be careful, but that doesn't make ignoring the simmering tension between Emily and me any easier, challenging every barrier I had so skillfully put into place.

# Chapter Three (Emily)

By the time Lucas finishes his conversation with Chloe at the front desk, I manage to compose myself, recovered from his close proximity as we reviewed my work. Well, mostly. My cheeks still burn at the memory of our first night together, his fingers tracing slowly, teasing circles over my skin, and the sight of him standing there now, so casually handsome, makes my pulse quicken.

I can't deny the chemistry between us, as much as I might want to. It was foolish of me to think one incredible night together wouldn't impact things or make our working relationship awkward. Lucas stirs something deep inside me, a hunger I've never known, and one that threatens to consume me whole if I'm not careful.

Which is why, when he wanders over a few minutes later, I paste on my most professional smile. "All set?" I ask briskly. "We should probably finish up if we want to review the latest offers before your next meeting."

"Right." Lucas clears his throat, shoving his hands in his pockets. He looks almost nervous, though I'm sure that's impossible. "Lead the way."

As we head back to his office, I feel the weight of his gaze on me. It takes every ounce of willpower not to turn and meet those deep blue eyes, to get lost once more in their depths.

This partnership is going to kill me, I just know it. But when it means staying close to Lucas, even in this limited capacity, it's a fate I'm willing to accept.

\#

After a couple weeks of getting the hang of working for him, I walk into Lucas's gym, the familiar scent of sweat and determination filling my senses. The space is empty this early, the mats freshly mopped and equipment gleaming under the fluorescent lights.

Lucas emerges from his office, wiping his hands on a towel. "You're early."

"I couldn't sleep." I shrug, avoiding his gaze.

"Me neither." He tosses the towel aside, his eyes darkening as he moves closer. "The marketing campaign is shit," he growls out of nowhere. "Who approved that garbage?"

I fold my arms, raising a brow. "You did. Last week."

He scowls, running a hand through his hair. "Well, I changed my mind."

"You can't just change your mind, Lucas. The digital ads are already running, and this campaign cost us nearly fifty grand."

He paces the area like a caged beast. "It's not your area of expertise. You shouldn't be involved in it."

Anger flares in my chest at his unreasonable behavior. "You hired me to give you my opinion, remember? To make sure you don't make stupid business decisions you'll regret later."

"I don't need a watchdog, Emily," he snaps. "I've been doing this for years without your help."

I suck in a sharp breath, stung. His eyes widen as if realizing his mistake, but the damage is done. Without another word, I turn on my heels, prepared to storm out of his gym, ignoring his call for me to come back.

Our fiery personalities and clashing approaches to business have led to more than one argument, but he has never snapped like this, out of nowhere. And he never insinuated I'm not needed before. I thought we were past this point, that he respected my role here.

"Emily, stop," he demands. But I ignore him, grabbing my coat. And just as I push on the door, his hand grips my shoulder. "Stop, please." His voice more of a whisper. "I'm an asshole. Can we just start again?"

I slow my pace and turn to look at him, ready to tell him to fuck off. But he looks tired, the lines around his eyes more pronounced. He's clearly going through more than I realize.

"Can we talk?" he asks.

I nod stiffly. "You want to talk more about the campaign? Now?"

"It's not about the campaign." He runs a hand through his hair with a sigh. "I owe you an apology. I was out of line, and I'm sorry."

Surprise flickers through me at his admission. "Oh."

"I shouldn't have implied you're not needed here. That was unfair, and untrue." His gaze lifts to mine, blue eyes piercing. "The truth is, I need your help. Please stay."

I know I should leave and not look back. He's too unpredictable and explosive. And at the same time, he's too charming and likable. It is a terrible combination. But I see the look in his eyes, the need for loyalty and support.

"Fine," I state, turning back.

His shoulders lower from their tense position at his neck. He takes my jacket and hangs it again.

Pressing his lips together, he finally says, "Are you worried about our upcoming negotiations?"

The quick switch back to business gives me whiplash.

"Not worried," I say. "Just focused."

He nods. "Same." And he glances at my clothing, as if assessing something. "Sounds like we could use some distraction, channel our intense focus elsewhere."

My brows knot together in confusion, sensing his returned arrogance oozing off of him.

Lucas walks into the middle of the mat, demonstrating a choke hold on an invisible sparring partner. His muscular arms flex as he secures the fake hold, and a wave of heat washes over me. I clench my jaw, pushing the unwanted attraction aside. We have work to do, and now is not the time to derail this partnership.

He signals for me to join him on the mat.

I shake my head, pushing off his invitation. "I wanted to get started." I tip my folders at him. "We have a lot to cover if we're going to make progress before the meeting." I grin, hoping he can't see the nerves twisting in my stomach.

"We can start by reviewing the contracts I've already secured and the details for expansion. But first, you look tense. You need a quick workout. It's time you learned a little about the art form you're representing." His lips quirk up on one side, a glint of challenge in his eyes. "Unless you're afraid you can't keep up?"

I scoff, indignation overshadowing my attraction. "In your dreams. Just because you're some big, bad military general doesn't mean I can't wipe the mat with you."

"Prove it." He holds up his hands, moving into a fighting stance. "Come at me with everything you've got."

My pulse leaps as I kick off my shoes and move onto the mat, mirroring his stance. Here we go again, letting our competitive natures get the better of us. But I can't back down from a challenge, and neither can he. This is the push and pull that both frustrates and thrills me. I just hope I don't do something I regret.

Like kissing that smug grin right off his face.

I strike fast, aiming a kick at his ribs that he deflects easily. He retaliates with a series of quick jabs I dodge by a hair's breadth, my heart pounding as I duck and weave around him.

"Too slow," he taunts, and it's all the motivation I need to attack again, fueled by irritation. Our bodies clash and grapple, each fighting for the upper hand, and I'm acutely aware of every point of contact between us. The strength in his hands as he grabs my wrists, the solid warmth of his chest against my back when he pulls me against him, his breath hot on my neck—

I wrench away with a growl, chest heaving as I put space between us. The sexual tension is unbearable, setting my nerves on fire, and I can see the same heat reflected in his eyes. I know he feels this pull as strongly as I do, no matter how much he tries to deny it.

"Well?" He raises an eyebrow, smugness radiating off him in waves. "Have I worn you out already?"

"In your dreams," I spit again, louder this time to cover the breathlessness in my voice. I launch myself at him once more and we grapple across the mats, each fighting for dominance we refuse to give over.

Until he pins me beneath him, my wrists captured above my head as he straddles my hips. Triumph gleams in his eyes and I buck against him, straining to break his hold, but it's no use. I'm caught fast in his grip, our bodies pressed together in a way that steals the breath from my lungs.

"Do you yield?" His voice is a low rumble against my ear, sending a shiver down my spine. I swallow hard, acutely aware of the position we're in, and the only thing I can think to yield to is the desire burning through my veins.

"Never," I grit out, just as the chimes above the door ring out.

In one swift move, Lucas is off me, reaching his hand to help me up, as a loud crash startles us and pulls our attention across the gym.

My jaw drops as I stare at Dom, standing there with a heavy dumbbell lying at his feet and a furious scowl twisting his features. His gaze zeroes in on Lucas, and then on me, and when he speaks, his voice is laced with venom.

"Well, isn't this cozy? I see you've wasted no time movin' on." His South Boston accent thick with anger.

"What the hell are you doing here, Dom?" I shoot out, causing Lucas's spine to straighten and his shoulders to square.

"Does he know you're just usin' him to get back at me?" Dom spits, shaking his head.

I blink, certain his attack can't be real, and I walk over to him, brows furrowed.

"Dom, why are you here? What's going on?" I hiss through clenched teeth, shocked by his presence.

His expression lightens as I get closer and regret washes across his eyes. "Sorry, I just saw your car out front and wanted to see you, I guess. I didn't expect to walk in on that." He gestures toward Lucas, who continues to watch our every move, wound tight.

"Well, you can't just waltz back into my life whenever you want," I say. "You're not going to like what you see. I've had to move on, Dom. You messed it all up."

"I know." He eyeballs Lucas, dropping his voice to a whisper, saying, "I was stupid, and I want to make it up to you." He reaches for my hand. "I want you to give me another chance."

I pull my hand away from his. "No, Dom, I'm not ready for that, for any of this." My jaw tenses. "I need you to leave. You can't just show up like this." Images of finding his lover's panties in our bed linens and him turning it on me, as if *his* cheating were *my* fault, sicken me.

He moves closer, into my personal space, and leans in. "No, Emily. You have to listen."

And before I can say a word, Lucas's voice booms from behind me.

"I believe she's asked you to leave," he growls, moving forward like a freight train, eyes flashing dangerously.

My hand instinctively moves up, reaching for Lucas's chest, pressing against him to hold him back. The effort of stopping his advance only riles Dom up more.

The tension in the room ratchets up another notch, both men radiating aggression.

"What the fuck? Is he your boyfriend now?" Dom spits, acting like he's been deceived.

"He's my boss, Dom," I say, tone rigid.

He nods, glancing at Lucas. "Ya, I bet he is," he says. "Just wait. You'll come crawling back to me soon enough," he calls over his shoulder, turning to leave. The door slams behind him, rattling the glass.

Silence falls over the gym, heavy and strained, as I release a shaky breath, scrubbing my hands over my face. What a hot mess.

A warm hand settles comfortingly against the small of my back, and I glance up to find Lucas watching me, a crease between his brows. His anger seems to have vanished, replaced by concern.

"Are you alright?" His voice is soft, gentle. It soothes the storm of emotions churning inside me.

I give him a weak smile. "I will be."

He pulls me into his arms without another word, wrapping me in the solid strength of his embrace. I cling to him, breathing in the clean scent of his skin and listening to the steady thump of his heart.

It's exactly where I want to be. Where I belong.

# Chapter Four (Lucas)

The gym buzzes with energy, the sound of heavy bags being pummeled and hands slapping mats filling the air. Sweat drips from my forehead as I watch my high-level fighters execute their jujitsu techniques with precision. Business is good, great even. Expansion plans are on the horizon, and I feel a hard-earned sense of pride in what I've built. But amidst all the success, there's a part of me that still feels broken.

"Lucas, I managed to finalize the lease agreement for the new location," Emily calls out, her voice cutting through the noise of the gym. I turn to see her approaching, clutching a thick stack of documents in her arms.

"Great work, Emily," I say, maintaining a professional tone, while inside, I can't believe how much she's helped me reach my goals. Her negotiation skills are unmatched, and she's never afraid to call me out when I'm being an asshole. She's a big reason why things are moving forward the way they are.

"Are you sure about this place? The rent is pretty steep," she says, raising an eyebrow. "I mean, I know we're expanding, but—"

"Trust me. It's worth the investment," I assure her, cutting off her concerns. As much as I value her opinion, I still need to know that I'm in control.

"Alright, if you say so," she sighs, handing me the documents. "Just remember, I'm here to help. You don't have to do everything on your own."

"Thanks," I reply curtly, avoiding eye contact. I can tell she's trying to break through, offering support that goes beyond her role here. But I hold back, fearing my inability to maintain control in the relationship realm.

As we pore over the documents together, I feel myself stealing glances at her. She's smart, sassy, and unapologetically opinionated—all traits that draw me closer to her, despite our differences. And she's beautiful as fuck. But for now, I need to stay focused on my growing empire and keep my distance from her.

I adjust the snug fit of my black rash guard, preparing to get on the mat with my best fighter. I notice Emily walk through the lobby and my eyes lock on her. A quick shake of my head clears my mind and I flex my toes, grounding them beneath me.

My attention quickly shifts as Xavier emerges from the locker room. The gym seems to come alive with his commanding presence. Standing tall and broad-shouldered, he exudes a formidable aura that demands respect. The razor-sharp focus in his dark eyes, black hair shadowing his face, gives him a hardened look that intimidates most of his opponents. But I know Xavier well, and behind his tough exterior, is a steady man he allows few to know.

Our eyes meet, and a knowing smile tugs at the corners of my lips. As he approaches, I extend my hand, and our palms come together in a firm clasp. "Ready to unleash the fire within, my friend?" I ask.

Xavier nods, his intense dark-brown eyes stirring with determination. "You bet, Lucas. You think today's the day to redeem yourself?"

His jab at his last win shoots adrenaline through my veins. He's the only one I can grapple with and allow to win without wanting to end him. He's a fair match and the only one in the dojo who's willing to give his all when fighting me.

"I won't let you off easy this time," I say. "Time to wipe that smug grin off your face." And I twist my body, stretching out my back.

Emily passes through the foyer again, glancing over at me as if she has something to tell me. I see her eyes move over my body, lingering, and she blinks, looking away, and heads back to the office. She hasn't seen me fight before and I wonder how it would affect her.

"She's got potential, you know," Xavier remarks casually as he stretches on the gym mat.

I grunt noncommittally, not quite ready to admit that I've been thinking the same thing. His mention of her, though, opens my eyes, knowing he has an uncanny way of reading people. He's noticed her fearlessness and quick wit when she challenges me, laughing at me like I'm whipped. And silently, I recognize her determination to break through my walls, just as Xavier does, and it's unsettling.

"Come on, man," he challenges, smirking as he takes his position across from me. "You can't deny that she brightens up the place whenever she's around."

"Alright, enough talk. Let's spar," I mutter, not wanting to expose my feelings about her just yet.

Our sparring session begins, our movements fluid and evenly matched, each of us anticipating the other's next move. As high-level black belts, we've trained together countless times, honing our advanced techniques and pushing each other to our limits.

"Seriously, Lucas," Xavier pants, grabbing my wrist as I attempt to pin him down. "She's not afraid to stand up to you, and she's got your back. That's pretty rare, man."

"Focus," I growl, twisting out of his grip and using his momentum against him, throwing him off balance. But even as we grapple and try to keep focus, I can't help but hear his words.

Finally, I manage to catch Xavier in a tight hold, my arm firmly around his neck while my legs wrap around his torso. He taps out, signaling his submission.

"Alright, alright," he concedes, gasping for breath as I release him. "Looks like I might have touched on a sensitive topic." He grins. "The one thing you're afraid of."

"Enough, asshole," I snap, my irritation flaring. "I came here to train, not discuss my love life."

"Ah, so you see it too," he laughs, a playful grin spreading across his face. "Just remember, man—sometimes, the best way to win is to let someone else in."

His words resonate with me as I watch him walk away, leaving me to grapple with how well he knows me and what he sees in Emily. I consider his words for a moment and the possibility that maybe, just maybe, she might be worth the risk. The thought intrigues me, but as I look over at her, laughing with some of the other gym members, I feel rage course through my veins, wanting to protect her and keep other men away from her. And it's clear to me, I'm just not cut out for this.

#

As I sit on the edge of the mat, catching my breath and wiping the sweat from my forehead, the gym door swings open, and Chloe saunters in with a bright smile for everyone she passes. Her eyes eventually land on Emily, and she makes a beeline for her.

"Hey, girl!" Chloe exclaims, throwing her arms around her in a tight embrace. "Ready for girls' night out?"

"Absolutely!" Emily replies, her face lighting up.

As they chatter excitedly, I walk over, listening intently to every word.

"Remember when we went skydiving with those ridiculously hot instructors?" Chloe asks, giggling and nudging Emily playfully. "When you nearly passed out midair."

"Don't remind me." Emily shakes her head. "What about it?"

"I got a random DM from their company, wanting us to schedule another jump." Her brows lift, anticipating an answer.

Emily took a step back. "I don't think so, Chloe. One jump is enough for me."

"Aww, don't be a downer," she presses. "It's better than spending all your free time at the dog shelter."

"Hey, don't hate on the shelter," Emily retorts, feigning offense as a blush creeps over her cheeks. "And that jump was nothing compared to the time we got backstage at Chris Stapleton and you threw up on my knee-high cowgirl boots!" She lets out a chuckle as Chloe punches her arm.

"Alright, fine. We're even," Chloe concedes, laughing along with Emily.

I watch their easy banter, their closeness, and a pang of longing hits me. What would it be like to share that level of intimacy with someone like Emily? But almost as quickly as the thought enters my mind, I dismiss it, reminding myself I'm better off alone.

"Sounds like you two could use some discipline," I chide mockingly, entering their space.

Emily turns towards me, raising an eyebrow. "Oh really? And who made you the fun police?"

"Hey, a little discipline never hurt anyone." I hope to redirect their evening to something more mellow.

"Sure." Chloe rolls her eyes, looping her arm through Emily's. "But neither did a little fun."

The tension in the room thickens as my jaw clenches, the unspoken challenge hanging heavy in the air. The thought of letting go, even if just for a moment, gnaws at me.

"Lucas, seriously," Emily says, her tone softening as she shifts her weight from one foot to the other. "When was the last time you did something fun outside of this gym?"

I narrow my eyes. "What are you suggesting?"

"Nothing," she replies innocently, a mischievous glint in her eyes. "I'm just saying, maybe you should take a break once in a while. Come out with Chloe and me sometime."

"Yeah, I don't think so," I scoff, trying to hide my immediate interest in the idea.

"Ugh, so regimented," Chloe exclaims, rolling her eyes. "Let loose for a bit. It might do you some good."

"Fine," I grumble, mostly to stop them, but partly because the prospect of spending more time with Emily may not be so bad. "We'll see."

"Great!" Chloe beams, her face lighting up with genuine excitement. "I haven't seen you relax those shoulders in years." She gave me a hug, reminding me of our years growing up together, always looking out for each other.

As I watch the two of them leave the gym, their laughter echoing through the empty space, I consider the possibility that they're right. Maybe taking a break from work—even if it's just for one night—could be worth it. And if it means getting to know Emily better, then perhaps it's a risk I'm willing to take.

# Chapter Five (Emily)

I step through the doors of Lucas's gym, my heart pounding with trepidation. This place has become a second home to me, a sanctuary where I can get away from the other parts of my freelance work. I'm struggling to find new clients and the dog shelter is pressuring me for more support on their non-profit negotiations. The gym is the one place I feel under control, except for maybe one thing.

My eyes catch Lucas's as he walks toward me. "Morning, Emily," he greets me with a warm smile, his piercing blue eyes meeting mine. "Ready to review the contracts?" He hands me a hot coffee, steaming in my favorite mug.

I nod, swallowing the nerves that threaten to unhinge me. This meeting holds huge significance for my future here, and I can't afford any missteps, but my focus has been so scattered from my other clients, I feel unprepared. As Lucas studies my work, he raises a few questions, probing deeper into the details. With each question, I can feel the weight of my mistakes, the shortcomings I had hoped to keep hidden.

"Well," Lucas says, a hint of concern etched on his face, "it seems like some of our opportunities are waffling. What's going on?"

I shift uncomfortably, my gaze momentarily dropping to the floor. "I think I've been trying to juggle too many responsibilities outside of the gym." I shake my head. "I'm hemorrhaging clients and spending time trying to dig up new ones."

Lucas's eyes hold disappointment, clearly wanting his gym to be my priority. But he knows how hard I've worked on building my career, not just with his enterprise. My stomach sours from the look on his face, knowing the gym is the only contact I truly care about.

He leans against the desk, folding his arms across his chest. "Emily, I've seen your dedication and potential. But you need to prioritize. If you want to succeed, you have to be fully committed."

His words stab me, a reminder of the choices I need to make, and of the things I need to cut and leave far behind me. Dom's attempts at contacting me continue to derail my progress. I keep blocking him, but he finds every way possible to reach me. And with Chloe's wedding plans moving forward, it's enough to make me want to crawl into a hole and hide. I know it's time to reassess my priorities and pour my energy into what truly matters, and I have to do it now.

"You're right," I say. "I need to focus more on strategy and removing distractions. Ugh, I just can't believe this." I look at my messages on my phone. "Another client just released me for some AI-driven marketing service," I vent, frustration building up inside, and I feel my face heat with embarrassment.

"Hey, don't worry about it," he says, his voice soothing like warm honey. "We'll figure something out to reduce your commitments outside of Walker Enterprises. I want your full focus. So, let's get you back on track and maybe restructure your business model."

I look into his eyes and feel a little calmer. It's not just his physical presence that makes me feel safe, there's something deeper, more genuine about him that I never expected to find in a man like him.

"Thanks," I say, my voice almost a whisper. "It's just not like me to see my business tanking. I didn't want you to have to see this."

"Look," he says, leaning forward, elbows on the table. "If anyone can figure this out, it's you."

I nod, attempting to believe him. "I just need to regroup. I have strong ideas for your contracts that will come together in the next day or two.

No worries, really. This is my priority." I pull back, not wanting him to see my weakness.

"Or, you know, you could let me help you," Lucas says, tipping his head, looking straight into my eyes.

#

As we dive into brainstorming ideas and strategies, I glance at him, sharp focus and intensity oozing off his broad shoulders, as he works on helping me reset my business plans. The last thing I ever expected was for him to act as a mentor, but for now, I'll take any support I can get.

"Alright, first things first," he begins, his eyes scanning my website on his laptop. "You need more visibility. I'll tell you what, you can use Walker Enterprises as a reference on your site. Having a well-known franchise backing you up might just give you the edge you need."

"That would be amazing," I agree, gratitude lacing my tone. "I can add it there," I point to the banner at the side, reaching over his hands on the keyboard.

"Exactly," he says. "Now, you need to focus on finding higher-paying clients. The effort at gaining new clients is the same, so why not go for the top ones?"

I nod, processing his strategy, knowing it makes perfect sense, but gaining access to the big deals is nearly impossible.

"A few high-end clients will replace several lower-paying ones, freeing up more of your time to do other things." He glances at me for a moment, then shifts his eyes back to the computer.

He starts searching online, and I watch as his fingers dance across the keyboard with surprising grace. He leans in closer to the screen, his brow furrowed in concentration, and I admire the way his muscles flex up his forearms. *Focus, Emily.*

"Here we go," he announces, snapping me back to reality. "I've found a few leads in my own contacts for potential clients who are looking for someone with your skillset. Why don't you reach out to them and see if they're interested? You can use my name as your referral."

"Lucas, this is incredible," I say, taking a look at the leads he's found. They seem like a perfect fit for my business, and I can already feel hope surging through me. "You're a lifesaver."

"Hey, it's the least I can do," he replies modestly. "Just promise me one thing, don't let them steal your true focus away from my business. I need you here."

His words send chills through me. "I promise Lucas," I say, feeling a renewed sense of determination.

#

A few days later, I find myself in Lucas's office, working on updating my website with the suggestions he gave me. With every piece of advice he offers or connection he shares, I can't deny that I'm seeing him in a new light. The air between us is electrified, and the tension hangs thick.

"Emily, let me show you something," he says as he guides me over to a corner of the gym that was recently renovated over the weekend. The space is sleek and modern, the perfect backdrop for a photoshoot.

"Wow, this looks amazing!" I gush, already envisioning how great the fighters will look posing there. "It's exactly what you envisioned."

As our eyes meet, I feel a shiver run down my spine. He's so close—close enough that I can see the rise and fall of his chest.

"Emily," Lucas murmurs. "You need to know that your influence here is making a difference. For the better."

"Thanks," I reply softly. "I really appreciate all of your support too."

We stand there for a moment, caught in each other's gaze, until Lucas abruptly steps back. His eyes are filled with an emotion I can't quite place—fear, maybe?

Then my phone lights up. My mechanic tells me he needs to order parts and my car won't be ready for pick up.

"Damn it," I murmur, knowing I'm expected at the shelter soon.

"What's up?" he asks, looking at my phone in my hand.

"It's just my car. It's being held hostage at Vinny's."

He nods knowingly. "Yup. He's known for that. Need a ride?"

"I'm actually headed to the dog shelter next," I say, shrugging my shoulders, preparing for him to make fun of me.

He glances at his watch. "I can take you."

"No, really, you don't have to. I can just call an Uber." I open the app on my phone.

He reaches and puts his hand over the screen. "Seriously. I'll take you. I'd like to see what all the hype's about."

"Really?" I stare at him in disbelief.

"Yeah, you can't be the only one around here trying out new things." He smirked. "I'm not one for pets or dogs, but I'm open to checking it out."

"Okay, then," I grab my bag and my jacket, unable to hide my smile. "Let's go."

I watch as he quickly has words with his gym manager, who nods and then returns his focus to the grappling fighters. Lucas grabs his keys from his desk and joins me, opening the door, allowing me to exit first.

I follow him to his sleek black SUV, and I hop in, immediately greeted by the scent of leather and the cool blast of air-conditioning.

"Nice ride," I comment as he pulls away from the curb.

"Thanks," he grins. "So where is this place? Tell me more about it. What do you do there?"

"Just head toward Castle Island. It's near the wharf. I'll show you." I point him in the right direction, and he turns, following my instructions. "I help mainly with walking, feeding, and playing with the dogs. Sometimes I assist with adoption events and review some of their non-prof contracts," I explain. "It can get emotional, you know, the dogs are so amazing, all needing homes. So I just give them as much love and affection as possible while they wait for their new forever families."

"Sounds interesting," he muses, putting his sunglasses on, making him look even sexier.

As we drive towards the shelter, sharing stories and laughter, I find myself drawn even closer to him. Not only is he supportive of my struggling business, but he's also curious and open-minded about my interests. I have to swat away the notion that there might be something growing between us, because, in truth, he's been clear with his signals for me to keep my distance.

Once we arrive, I lead Lucas through the entrance of the dog shelter, the chorus of barks and wagging tails filling the air. Jayne, at the front desk, welcomes me and I introduce her to Lucas, his focus already drawn down the row of kennels. Jayne smirks at me, ogling at his back as he follows the barks, and I shake my head at her and roll my eyes.

"I've never been to a place like his before," he admits, looking at all the cages with curiosity.

I smile, excited to share this part of my life with him. "Welcome to my world, Lucas. You're gonna love this."

As we walk down the aisles, the dogs clamor for attention, their eyes pleading for love and companionship. Lucas's military background is etched in the lines of his face, his stiff, formal posture, and I sense the weight he carries. I have a feeling these dogs will sense it too and might just be what his soul needs.

We approach a kennel, and a gentle-eyed, black Labrador mix named Charlie greets us with a wagging tail. I open the door, allowing Lucas to step inside and interact with the dog. Charlie leans into Lucas's touch, his eyes shining with a mixture of trust and gratitude. They hold eye contact without blinking as if communicating in silence.

"He's amazing," Lucas says, his voice filled with awe. "He just seems to... understand."

I nod, knowing exactly what he means. "They offer unconditional love and companionship, no matter what you've been through. Never any judgment."

Lucas's gaze lingers on Charlie, and I can see a flicker of relief in his eyes. The weight of his military trauma seems to momentarily fade away in the presence of this furry friend. It's a small moment of solace that seems to soothe his tormented soul.

"Thank you, Emily," he says softly. "For bringing me here." His voice catches in his throat.

"You're welcome," I respond. "Though it was your idea." I chuckle. "But I just knew these dogs would like you. They're amazing like that."

We spend the afternoon at the shelter, Lucas's presence bringing comfort and joy to the dogs we encounter. With each interaction, I see him finding a renewed sense of purpose. And as we leave, I feel lighter than I have in weeks. The stress of my struggling business momentarily forgotten, replaced by comfortable chat and simply sharing space.

"Thanks for joining me today," I say as we approach his car. "And for the ride."

"No problem," he says with a grin. "I honestly didn't expect it to be that cool."

"Oh, okay. I *can* be cool, you know," I tease.

He chuckles, "Yeah. I guess."

I roll my eyes and shake my head, and we arrive back at the gym, still talking about Charlie's happy wiggle. As he pulls into his space, I see Chloe pacing impatiently near the entrance. Her arms are crossed over her chest, and she taps her foot in irritation.

"Emily! Where have you been?" she calls as soon as we're within earshot. "I've been waiting for an hour!"

"Sorry, Chloe," I apologize sheepishly. "I didn't expect you so soon. We lost track of time at the shelter." I feel bad knowing she wanted to go dress shopping.

Her gaze shifts between Lucas and me, her eyes narrowing. "The dog shelter?" She looks at Lucas in confusion. "You don't even like dogs."

"It was actually amazing, Chloe. My eyes have been opened." And he looks at me with a smile.

Her expression turns to a frown as she sees the comfortable energy between us. "I see. Leave it to Emily to open your eyes." Her tone stung with sarcasm. "Well, I'm glad you two had a nice time together, but maybe you should focus on your contacts instead of frolicking with dogs."

My chin pulls in from her unexpected negativity.

"Chloe, he needed the break," I protest, feeling a rush of heat to my cheeks. "Lucas and I have been working all morning, and I needed a ride to the shelter." I notice my defensive stance and soften it. "And the dogs are a perfect distraction."

"Really, Emily? Defending him?" she says skeptically, her eyes flickering to Lucas. "And what's in it for you?"

"Nothing," he replies coolly. "Just helping out a friend."

"Right," Chloe snorts, clearly not buying it. She turns to me, her voice nearly a whisper, saying, "Emily, I just don't want you to get hurt again. Dom has left fresh wounds. You need time."

My jaw clenches at the sound of Dom's name, and from her attempt at using him against me. She'd already made herself perfectly clear that she was shocked to see Lucas and me together outside of our work with the gym. But it was not her place to be so bold about her opinions. I'd have to talk with her more about where this was all coming from, privately.

# Chapter Six (Lucas)

I try to keep my cool with Chloe, but her sudden ambush as Emily and I returned from the dog shelter was unexpected, triggering my pulse to rise almost instantly. My clenched jaw helped to hold back any emotional response, but as soon as she turned on Emily, bringing up her ex as a weapon, I feel myself losing emotional control.

"Lucas!" Chloe's voice cuts like a knife, sharp and unexpected. She storms toward us, fury written all over her usually bubbly face. "What do you think you're doing?"

"You need to calm down," I say, my body tensing as she approaches like a tornado. The suddenness of her assault triggers something deep within me, sending my heart rate skyrocketing. Sweat beads on my forehead, and I find it difficult to breathe. It's as if I'm back on the battlefield, facing an enemy attack.

"Chloe, what's going on?" Emily asks, her tone confused. "Did something happen? You seem more upset about this than you should be." She steps between us like a shield. Her protective instinct only heightens my tension, proving there's a threat upon us.

"I know what's happening here. It's not hard to see," she snaps at Emily, then turns her glare on me. "You guys need to keep this strictly professional. I should never have suggested this partnership in the first place." She shakes her head, lips pressed together.

"Chloe, we're all adults here. You have nothing to worry about," Emily retorts, but her words barely register as my fight response claws at my insides. My emotions spiral out of control, and my temper flares like wildfire.

"You need to back off," I growl at Chloe, my fists clenching involuntarily. "I don't need you telling me how to spend my time."

All I can focus on is the rapid thud of my heart in my chest, the way it feels like I'm suffocating under the weight of my past. And then the betrayal, the last person I ever expected to send me into such a spiral was Chloe.

"So back the fuck off," I snarl through gritted teeth, barely recognizing my own voice. "You've crossed a line with your controlling bullshit, and I need you to stay far away from me now, out of my life." I step closer, chest out, creating an intimidating stance to push her away. The scowl on my face leaves no question that she's in danger if she continues to push.

A wave of hurt and disbelief flashes across her face, but she doesn't say another word. Instead, she storms away, leaving Emily and me standing in the parking lot in silence.

My body is tensed like a tightly wound spring. I tremble uncontrollably, my heart rate soaring through the roof as I struggle to draw in much-needed breaths. Emily stares at me as we stand in the parking lot, Chloe storming away from us. Chloe's ambush has us both rattled, but I know my response has already hit levels that I can't control.

"Lucas, are you okay?" Emily studies my face as I try to hide my fight instincts. "Your pupils are really dilated."

"I'm fine," I manage to choke out, the words barely escaping my lips. My vision blurs as I try to focus on her worried expression.

"Lucas, please, let me help you," she says, her voice trembling just as much as my body. I can see the concern etched on her face, but all I can think about is how I don't want to drag her into this mess—into my chaos.

"Emily, I..." My words trail off, the torrent of emotions inside me threatening to overwhelm me completely. It's a struggle just to breathe, let alone speak.

"Come on," her voice is gentle but firm as she leads me into the gym. "Let's get you to your office."

I follow her, my legs feeling like rubber beneath me. My eyes dart around nervously, taking in the gym that I once knew like the back of my hand. Now, it feels foreign and unfamiliar—every shadow a potential threat, every sound making me flinch.

"Don't trip on the gym bags," Emily warns, guiding me around the pile with a steady hand on my arm. Her touch is warm and comforting, a lifeline amidst my blind rage.

A sense of shame from my reaction to Chloe's ambush covers me, as the scent of sweat and sounds of sparring redirect my senses to a more familiar balance. I notice Xavier at the far side of the gym, watching with curiosity, and his presence grounds me further.

"Here we are," Emily says, opening the door to my office. She guides me to the leather couch against the wall and sits down beside me, our thighs touching.

"Take a deep breath. Focus on your breathing for a moment, okay?" Her voice is soft and soothing, pulling me back from the edge of panic.

I do as she says, closing my eyes and inhaling deeply, then exhaling slowly.

"Better?" she asks after a moment.

"A little," I admit, opening my eyes to find her studying me intently. "Emily, I... I haven't told you everything. About my PTSD, I mean."

"You don't have to explain," she reassures me, her hand resting gently on my forearm.

"No, I want to. I need to," I insist. "It's not like me to lose it like that. I usually have better control of my... situation." I drop my gaze to the floor. "I've just been having nightmares lately, so I'm a bit sleep deprived. They're so vivid like I'm right back in the thick of it—gunfire, explosions, people screaming." I take a breath. "And then, when something unexpected happens, like Chloe's attack, there are flashbacks.... One second I'm here, and the next, I'm reliving some of the worst moments of my life."

"Makes sense," she says, listening intently. "I'm so sorry this is happening to you."

"Sometimes, I just... I lose control," I continue, the words tumbling out of me now. "Like with Chloe. My temper flares, and I can't seem to rein it in. And other times, I feel completely numb, like I'm hollow inside." She squeezes my arm gently. "It's not just Chloe," I say hesitantly, feeling the weight of my recent troubles bearing down on me. "Sure, she triggered it, but there's something else, a competitor, threats."

"What do you mean, threats?" she asks, eyes filled with concern.

"His name is Carlo. We've always been rivals. And now he's trying to poach some of my prized fighters. He even went as far as saying he'll destroy my business." As I speak, the anxiety that has been gnawing at the back of my mind moves to the surface. "I've worked so hard to build this place, and now it feels like everything I've built is slipping through my fingers."

"No, you're not going to lose anything," she says, voice firm. "You're too strong. Capable. We'll figure this out together. But for now, you need to take care of yourself."

Her support is helpful, but I can feel my heart rate picking up again, the stress and anxiety tightening their grip on me.

"Your breathing is getting faster," she observes, her hand still resting on my arm. "Sit up straight and put one hand on your chest and the other on your stomach," she instructs. "Now, take a deep breath, making sure your diaphragm expands and not just your chest."

I follow her instructions, feeling odd but relieved to have something to focus on other than my own racing thoughts.

"Good," she says, her voice steady. "Now hold your breath, and then exhale slowly through your mouth."

I do as she says, concentrating on each breath, feeling the tension in my body start to dissipate with every controlled exhale.

"Keep going," she whispers. "Just focus on your breathing, Lucas. Remember that you're here, safe, and you're not alone."

My heart rate slows, my muscles relax, and the anxiety that had been threatening to swallow me whole recedes. As I continue to breathe deeply, the world outside fades away, leaving just Emily and me in our own world.

It's in that serene moment, my breath finally under control, that the door to my office swings open, and Xavier strides in. His gaze flicks between Emily and me—her hand still resting on my arm, our faces close—a small smile playing at the corners of his lips.

"Hey, boss," he says, leaning against the doorframe. "Looks like I came just in time for the group therapy session." The humor in his voice helps my frayed nerves.

"Xavier," I acknowledge with a nod, knowing he understands what just went down.

"Well, thank you, Emily." His eyes soften as he looks at her. "Looks like you've got the magic touch when it comes to calming our fearless leader here."

"Call it intuition," she replies, her cheeks tinge pink, but her expression remains genuine.

"Well, you've certainly got that," Xavier agrees, giving me a knowing glance. It's clear he believes Emily is good for me. And if I'm honest with myself, I can't deny the truth in that.

"Anyway, I'll leave you two to it," he says, pushing away from the doorframe. "Just remember, Lucas, you've got people who care about you, man. Don't forget that."

"Thanks, Xavier," I manage, my throat still tight.

He offers one last friendly nod before slipping back out of the room, leaving Emily and me alone again.

Swallowing hard, I let the vulnerability rise to the surface, my heart pounding in my chest. "I just... I can't lose you, Emily. Not now when everything else feels like it's falling apart."

"Hey," she says softly, her thumb gently brushing over my knuckles. "Don't listen to Chloe. She doesn't control me either. You don't have to worry, okay? I'm not going anywhere." I nod, the fear of abandonment clawing at my insides. "I promise," she reassures me, her eyes never leaving mine.

## Chapter Seven (Emily)

I sit in Lucas's office, recalling our recent interaction here when I helped him come down from his panic attack, but this time it's me with a phone pressed against my ear, trying to convince a potential client that our partnership would be beneficial. I feel Lucas's eyes on me, tense and expectant. He wants this negotiation to go well—we both do.

"Absolutely, Mr. Chamime," I say, injecting as much charm and confidence into my voice as possible. "Our combined efforts would create a synergy that's unparalleled in the MMA industry. With our expertise in training top fighters and your marketing resources, the growth and visibility would be exponential."

I glance at Lucas, who's perched on the edge of his desk, arms crossed over his broad chest. His jaw is clenched, a subtle sign of his anxiety.

It's strange to see him like this, considering his usual unshakeable confidence. But this deal means a lot for his business growth into Dubai.

"Of course, Mr. Chamime," I continue, scribbling notes on the pad in front of me. "We appreciate your concerns and will ensure all necessary precautions are taken to uphold the integrity of your brand. Our main goal is to raise visibility by winning, in all arenas."

Lucas's gaze never leaves me, but I can tell he's impressed by the way he raises an eyebrow and nods subtly. I smile inwardly, knowing that my ability to navigate complex negotiations with finesse contrasts well with his no-nonsense military-trained mindset.

"Thank you, Mr. Charmime," I say, cringing at my slight mispronunciation of his name, wrapping up the call. "We'll have our proposal to you by tomorrow morning. Have a great day."

I hang up the phone and let out a long breath, turning to face Lucas. The tension in the room seems to dissipate slightly now that the call is over. I feel a little proud of how it went, and I'm eager for his reaction.

"So, uh," he begins, a smile playing at the corner of his lips. "You handled that like a pro."

I beam at his praise, feeling a warmth spread through my chest. It's nice to know that he appreciates my skills and trusts me to handle such an important call.

"Thanks, Lucas," I reply, trying to keep my voice steady despite the sudden flutter in my stomach. "That means a lot coming from you."

He leans back against the desk, surveying me with admiration in his eyes. For a moment, the air between us feels charged, but I shake off the feeling, reminding myself of our promise to keep things professional.

"Let's get to work on that proposal," I suggest, picking up my pen again.

Lucas nods but then clears his throat with a slight smirk on his lips. "So, I had no idea we were branching out into the toilet paper industry with Mr. Charmin."

My cheeks immediately flush as I recall the embarrassing name slip-up, but I can't help but laugh. "Asshole." I stand and throw my pen at him.

He catches it playfully, only making him more attractive.

"Alright, alright," I concede, holding up my hands in mock surrender. "Everyone makes mistakes. And you can't deny it's not a bad product."

"True," he chuckles. "But you have to admit, it was pretty funny."

"Only because you're teasing me about it now," I shoot back. Lucas raises an eyebrow, clearly enjoying himself. So, I continue. "And how does it feel to leave your military days behind and become a... super-soft toilet paper spokesperson? Your fighters can wear the logo on their rash guards." I laugh at my own joke.

He holds back at first, turning red, but then his laughter booms through the office, and I can't help the smile that spreads across my face at the sight of him doubled over, clutching his stomach. The sound is contagious, and soon we're both laughing so hard that tears prick at the corners of my eyes.

"Alright, you got me there," Lucas concedes, wiping away his tears. "But you have to admit, it would be quite the change of pace."

"Definitely," I agree, taking a deep breath to calm myself.

He suddenly becomes serious. "You're amazing at what you do, and I'm glad we're working together." His eyes hold mine, gaze growing more intense.

The air between us crackles with electricity as he moves to lock the office door, the sound of fighters grappling on the mats in the background. I can feel my heart pounding, anticipation coursing through me as he turns back to face me.

"Emily," he murmurs. "It might be time to break Chloe's rules."

He closes the distance between us in a heartbeat, and hovers in my personal space.

"I don't know," I tease. "She's such a stickler for rules."

"I used to be too," he whispers, moving even closer. "But somehow, I'm ready to throw them out the window."

I drop my papers onto the couch behind me and hold his gaze, waiting for his move.

And then it comes, in a swift motion of strength and desperation. His hand reaches around my neck as his fingers move into my hair, gripping and tilting my head back. I grab hold of his biceps to steady myself as his lips meet mine in a searing, passionate kiss, leaving me breathless.

His mouth searches mine, as he pulls me close, intoxicating me with his strong hold and his alluring masculine scent. Our earlier laughter is forgotten as we lose ourselves in each other, irresistibly drawn together despite our glaring differences.

I pull away, heart racing, and look up into his striking blue eyes. "I have to tell you something," I whisper, unable to tear my gaze from his.

"Anything," he replies, his voice husky.

"I've wanted this for a long time," I confess, laying my feelings bare. "Since I first met you, I wanted more. I can't explain it." The feel of his breath on my lips makes me crazy.

Lucas studies me for a moment, his eyes searching mine as if looking for something hidden within. He finally leans in, kissing me again, opening my lips with his, exploring me with his tongue. His hands cradle my face, thumbs brushing against my cheeks. My heart races, and I can't help but think that there's something deeper behind this kiss—something he's not saying.

"Emily," he murmurs between kisses, pulling back just enough so our lips barely touch. "I'm not good with words, but...."

"It's okay," I say softly, quieting him with my lips.

He hesitates for a heartbeat, then nods, giving in to the desire that's been building between us. As we continue kissing, our bodies pressed tightly together, he guides me back toward the couch. Our movements are slow and deliberate, each touch sending shivers down my spine.

We sink into the cushions, our bodies tangled, our mouths never breaking contact. I feel an overwhelming need to be close to him, to know every inch of his body, to see the man behind the hardened exterior. He seems to sense it too, his hands exploring my curves, leaving a trail of heat in their wake.

"Are you sure about this?" he asks, his voice thick with desire. "I don't want to get you into any trouble with Chloe." He smirks, but his eyes hold sincerity.

"Lucas," I reply, my voice steady despite the whirlwind of emotions coursing through me. "I've never been more sure of anything in my life."

In that instant, any remaining barriers between us crumble away. We lose ourselves in each other, as our clothes come off and he slides me beneath him. He kisses me further, then moves down, exploring my breasts with his mouth, teasing my nipples with his tongue, sending my arousal through the roof.

Feeling his muscles rippling beneath my touch, I let out a gasp as he enters me, thrusting his force into me as his eyes hold mine, unblinking. Every nerve in my body explodes from the feel of him, causing a surge of intensity to wash over me. He lets out a groan from deep within, sending me higher, and as we become one in our intimate connection, the world erupts and shifts, settling into new possibilities.

The rhythmic pounding of fists on heavy bags and the grunts of exertion reverberate through the gym, a stark reminder of the moment we've just shared. Lucas's breath is warm against my skin as he pulls away from me, his eyes searching mine.

"Shit," he mutters under his breath as the sound of a sharp whistle pierces the air. He knows he's needed out there, but I can't help the pang of uncertainty that shoots through me as he hastily zips his pants, eyes darting toward the door.

"Hey," he murmurs, catching my expression. He leans in, pressing a sweet, reassuring kiss to my lips. "Don't overthink it. Give me a few minutes, and I'll be right back."

With one last lingering look, he slips out of the office, leaving me to bask in the afterglow of our intimacy. The sounds of the gym continue to filter through the walls, but they're nothing compared to the raw memories of our passionate encounter. I replay the moans Lucas tried so hard to muffle, feeling his body spasm over mine again as my name passed his quivering lips, and heat rises in my cheeks.

As reality slowly seeps back in, I reach for my phone. My heart sinks when I see a text from the client we spoke with earlier—they're having second thoughts about the deal already. On top of that, there are several messages from Chloe, each more frantic than the last, wondering why neither Lucas nor I have been responding to her texts.

"Damn it," I whisper, torn between frustration and annoyance. I know I need to address the client's concerns, but at the same time, I can't ignore my best friend's panic.

I quickly type out a response to Chloe, assuring her that everything is fine and promising to call her soon, guilt hidden beneath each letter. Then, taking a deep breath, I turn my attention to the client's message, preparing to put out some fires.

But all the while, the one thing that claims my true focus is the energy lingering in my muscles from Lucas's body on mine.

# Chapter Eight (Lucas)

I slam the door to my office, a surge of frustration coursing through me. Negotiations with the Dubai deal are at a standstill, and I can't seem to find a way around it. Walker Enterprises is reliant upon sealing this contract if I want my business to make a monumental global impact. My fighters deserve the opportunity to compete for world championship belts and are definitely good enough to crush the competition.

Emily looks up from her laptop, concern etched on her face. "Everything okay?" she asks.

My shoulders droop with defeat as I take stock of the wall of my office. The endless whiteboards contain mounds of sticky notes that I've written in an attempt to solve the problems plaguing me. There's a hole in the wall where I threw a chair across my office last week during another failed brainstorming session. My tense staff is standing by but champing at the bit for action; they can smell that we're on the brink of being knocked out of contention for next year's championships.

"Everything's falling apart," I groan, the frustration surging like a tidal wave within me. My fingers sweep across my face, grating against the stubble on my chin, a futile attempt to scrub away the grit of worry and fatigue that has been torturing me these past few days.

It feels like I'm trying to put together a thousand-piece puzzle with half the pieces missing. The strategy, the training regimen, even the damn team chants—they all seem to be in shambles.

I can almost taste the disappointment as I visualize my team in Dubai, unprepared and disjointed, their dreams of victory evaporating. It's a bitter pill to swallow and I feel its sting, a relentless throb at the back of my skull.

I make an effort to anchor myself, to find that inner calm that had always been my ally in the face of adversity. I can't afford to let my temper spill over, to taint the air between us. Emily doesn't deserve the backlash of my frustration, the collateral damage of my internal storm.

With a deep sigh, the words tumble out once more. "Nothing's working," I repeat, the bitter edge to my voice more pronounced. The walls of the gym suddenly feel too confining, like they're closing in, suffocating me. "I need some air," I manage to say, my eyes already darting toward the exit.

A trace of a smile lifts her lips, not quite reaching her eyes, but it's there. It's like she's read my mind. Her intuition is uncanny, always seeming to guide me through the storms.

For a moment, I hesitate, my eyes never leaving hers. There's a warmth in her company, a comfort that I've come to lean on during times like these. But do I want to drag her into my turmoil, and shade her mood with my frustrations?

She seems to sense my inner struggle, her smile widening just a bit. And suddenly, the answer is clear.

"Sure," I respond. There's a small nod of my head, almost imperceptible, but it's there. It's an acceptance, an acknowledgment of her offer. And with it, the realization that her company, far from being a burden, might just be what I need right now. "I could use the company," I add, my voice rough around the edges but sincere. It wouldn't just be "not terrible"—it would be a welcome relief.

Without hesitation, we grab our jackets, their familiar weight comforting against the light chill of the late afternoon. We vacate the gym, the well-worn doors creaking shut behind us as we step into the brisk

Downtown air. It's a refreshing contrast to the heavy, sweat-laden atmosphere of the dojo we've just left behind, humming with the high-tension grind of grit and determination.

As we walk, the sun is dipping low in the sky, its fading light casting a radiant golden hour over the cityscape. It washes over the historic buildings lining the streets, their time-worn bricks glowing, their shadows stretching long and soft on the cobblestone paths. The scent of old stone and fresh evening air mingles with the faint aroma of street food wafting from a nearby vendor, the rich smell of grilled meats and onions tantalizing our senses.

As we navigate the labyrinth of streets, our strides naturally fall into sync. Our conversation flows easily, a mix of words and laughter that helps to soothe my frayed nerves. It's a reset, a grounding moment amidst the swirl of my nagging anxieties.

"Look at that," Emily exclaims. She points towards the Common where a street performer is juggling flaming torches. The firelight dances off his face, illuminating his features in an erratic, mesmerizing display of shadows and light.

"That guy's completely nuts," she says, shaking her head. The crackle and hiss of the fire cut through the cool evening air and just miss his hair every time.

"Definite insanity," I reply with a smirk. "Not all that different from what you do on a daily basis. Particularly with me as your boss."

Her laughter rings out, and I can't help but join in, feeling something inside me returning to life.

We continue our leisurely stroll along the cobblestone paths of Beacon Hill. The old gas lamps that line the streets flicker to life, their soft glow casting a romantic charm over the historic neighborhood. The faint aroma of fresh bread from a nearby bakery wafts up to us, mixed with the musty allure of old books from a tucked-away bookshop.

"Isn't it amazing how something so simple can be so beautiful?" she murmurs, looking up at the gas lamps. I nod, but I'm not really looking at the lamps anymore.

We eventually reach the edge of the Public Garden, where the Swan Boats lazily glide through the water. We watch a group of tourists excitedly clamber aboard, snapping pictures and waving. I roll my eyes.

"Have you ever ridden on one of those?" I ask with a straight face. "I know how much you like to live on the wild side."

"Lucas, please," she scoffs. "I'm more of a Duck Boat Tours girl." Her lips pull into a grin. "I assume you're the same, being a Navy SEAL and all... you know, the amphibious thing."

"True. True," I agree, our laughter filling the air between us.

Just then, out of the corner of my eye, I spot Carlo, the local competitor threatening to poach my prized fighters from the gym. He saunters over with an infuriating smirk plastered across his face. My jaw clenches, adrenaline flooding my system as he approaches, eyeing Emily like she's prey.

Every instinct in my body screams at me to protect her, but I know that if I move too quickly it will only make matters worse. Instead, I keep still and focus on staying calm during what could easily become an explosive situation.

"Hey, Lucas. Taking a break from the business?" he drawls, barely sparing me a glance before turning to Emily. "And who is this lovely lady? Your new master negotiator I've been hearing about?"

She hesitates, sensing the tension in the air and carefully choosing her words. "I'm Emily, helping Lucas with some business matters."

"Ah, such modesty," he coos, stepping closer to her, invading her personal space. I clench my fists so tightly my knuckles turn white, every instinct in my body screaming to protect her.

"Carlo," I hiss, my fists clenching tight. Taking a step closer to him, I glare and clench my jaw. "Get the hell away from her. I swear to God if you don't show her some respect...."

He takes a step back, but it's too late—his smug smirk has been firmly planted on his face. His gaze lingers on Emily for longer than necessary before he finally turns away. Something about the way he looks at her sets off alarms in my brain, making me want to take a swing at him even more.

"Of course, I wouldn't want to come between you," he sneers. He leans in closer to her, his voice dripping with false sweetness. "It was a pleasure meeting you, Emily. Maybe we'll run into each other again soon."

I feel my blood boiling as he turns and saunters away, that smug grin never leaving his face. I take a deep breath, trying to calm myself, knowing that reacting with violence would only serve to give him what he wants.

Emily's face contorts into a look of contempt as she watches him walk away. She crosses her arms tightly across her chest. "What a dick," she scoffs.

And I burst out laughing, releasing the built-up tension. "Exactly," I say. "Total dick."

She smiles and her hand gently brushes against mine. "Let's not let him ruin our afternoon, alright?" She gives me a small encouraging smile, and I know she's right. Carlo isn't worth our time or energy.

I intertwine our fingers, focusing on the warmth of her hand in mine, grounding myself in her presence.

"Come on," I say, trying to keep my voice steady, "let's walk."

As we move away, I can't help but replay his words in my head. That smug grin, his idle threats, the way he looked at Emily—it all fuels the fire inside me. But I know I need to keep myself calm, for both me and for Em.

"Don't let him get to you," she says softly, her voice pulling me back into the present. "That's what he wants. It's part of his strategy."

She glances at me, her big green eyes sparkling in the sun as she lifts an eyebrow. She knows exactly how to pull me out of this tailspin I find myself in.

"Easy for you to say," I mutter, though her words ring true. "That asshole's been trying to entice Xavier and some of my other top fighters to join his franchise. He's got some money and corporate backing to seduce them to his side."

She brushes a lock of hair behind her ear, meeting my eye with a resolute look. "Well, so do you. And plus, they would never leave you," she says without hesitation. "Especially Xavier. That man has your back more than anyone I've ever seen."

I glance down at her, my anger momentarily subsiding as I realize just how much her words mean to me. And in that moment, I find the courage to be honest with her.

"Emily, about what happened in my office...," I begin, hesitating briefly. "I know we haven't talked about it, but I want you to know that it meant something. I just never thought I'd meet someone like you or be able to navigate it."

She squeezes my hand gently, a small smile playing at the corners of her lips. "Well, I like you too, Lucas," she says plainly.

# Chapter Nine (Emily)

I glance over at Lucas, his muscular frame glistening with sweat as he spars with Xavier on the gym mat. I can't help but admire the way his muscles flex and move in perfect harmony, but there's no time for daydreaming now. My phone buzzes in my hand, and I recognize the number as the Dubai agent I've been waiting to hear from all week.

I step out of the gym, leaving the sounds of grunts and thuds behind as I answer the call.

"Hello?" I say, trying to ignore the clamor of the gym behind me.

"Emily? It's Rashid from Dubai. Do you have a moment to talk about the contract?"

"Of course," I reply, my heart pounding in excitement and nerves. Mr. Chamime introduced himself on a first-name basis, so that's a good sign.

This is it—the deal that could change everything for both Lucas's company and my own.

As the conversation intensifies, I pace back and forth, gesturing wildly as I negotiate terms and conditions. I'm so caught up in the call that I don't notice Lucas slip out of the gym and approach me, curiosity etched across his handsome face.

"Alright, we have a deal," I say into the phone, relief and triumph washing over me. "Thank you, Rashid." I hang up, taking a deep breath to steady myself before turning to face Lucas.

"Who was that?" he asks, his voice sharp and accusatory. He steps closer, towering over me like a protective bear. "You should have waited for me. What are you doing behind my back?"

His tone sets me off immediately, turning my elation to fury. Within one second, he accuses me of moving forward without him and doing business behind his back, or worse. Staring into his face, I see red.

"Back the fuck up, Lucas!" I snap, anger flaring instantly. "I'm doing my job and you just need to fuck off with that attitude." I press my finger into his chest, pushing him out of my space, fully expecting him to remain as immovable as a brick wall. But to my surprise, my gesture is enough to make him take a step back, eyes wide in surprise at my response.

We both stare at each other in shock for a moment and then laughter erupts between us as we recognize how foolish we're being.

"Okay, okay," I say, catching my breath. "First of all, I wasn't doing anything behind your back. That was the Dubai agent I've been talking to about our contract. And second, I can take care of myself. You don't need to be breathing down my neck every time I make a phone call."

Lucas's eyes soften, and he takes another step back, giving me space. "I'm sorry. I just worry about you sometimes."

"Thanks, but I can handle myself," I reply, a teasing smile tugging at the corners of my lips. "*Sooo*, we won the contract," I add.

"Seriously?" His eyes widen in astonishment. "Holy shit, Em. That's incredible!" He pulls me into a hug, lifting me off my feet briefly before setting me back down.

"Hey, you doubted my negotiation skills?" I tease, raising an eyebrow.

"Never," he replies, grinning. "And I have to admit, you've changed the trajectory of my company, and I couldn't be more grateful. How about we celebrate? Drinks on me."

\#

As we walk toward Castle Island, in search of my favorite pub, we admire the panoramic views of Boston Harbor, with sailboats gliding across the water and the distant skyline as the dramatic backdrop. The Southie neighborhood comes alive around us as we pass iconic triple-decker houses, rows of brownstone buildings, and locals chatting on their front stoops. The sun is beginning to set, causing the narrow, Irish pub-lined streets to sparkle.

Making our way toward Broadway, my favorite locale, Lucas watches a group of kids kick a soccer ball in a nearby park, their laughter carrying on the gentle breeze. A shadow moves across his face as if time stands still.

"Are you okay?" I ask, leaning forward to see into his eyes.

"Makes me think of my Navy buddy, Jack," he murmurs. "Always had a soccer ball, juggling it on his knees, while the rest of us watched the horizon for snipers."

I look out toward the kids, allowing him space to talk.

"He was from around here." He glances around. "I saved his ass more times than I can count when we were deployed together." He let out a slow exhale. "But it was Jack who made the ultimate sacrifice." He paused, staring into oblivion. "Pushed me out of the way as he spotted a landmine, triggering it to explode." He fell silent.

Without hesitation, I reach my arms around him and hold on. I hold him together with all my strength, pouring my love into him, praying it will help.

Listening to his heartbeat in my ear, my breath falls into rhythm with his, and we stay like that for a while. Then he reaches for my arms, moving them from around his ribs, and he holds my hands. Looking into my eyes, he reaches down and kisses me.

"Thanks," he whispers, then turns and starts walking toward our destination, keeping my hand firmly entwined in his.

As we continue our walk-through Southie toward my favorite bar, I feel grateful for this moment, for the unlikely partnership that brought us together and the undeniable chemistry that keeps pulling us closer.

Pushing through the heavy wooden doors of Broadway, we're instantly enveloped by the warm atmosphere, dim lighting, worn wooden tables, and regulars laughing loudly as they clink their glasses together.

"Wow, this place has character," Lucas remarks, taking in the mix of patrons and the various vintage signs adorning the walls.

"Isn't it great?" I beam, proud to show off my favorite place in Southie. "They have the most amazing selection of beers and whiskeys." We move closer to the bar.

"Today calls for something special," he declares, flagging down a server. "Champagne, please. We're celebrating an incredible victory."

"Yes, sir," the server replies, disappearing behind the bar.

"Are you okay here for a minute? I need to hit the Gents," Lucas says, turning toward the men's room as I nod with a smile. No sooner has he left, than I feel a familiar presence behind me. Turning around, I find myself face-to-face with Dom. His eyes are full of sweetness, but I sense a hint of desperation lurking beneath the surface.

"Emily, you following me?" he teases, moving closer. "You look amazing, baby." He leans in as if smelling my hair.

"Back off, Dom," I say, putting a hand up to set my boundary, noticing the smell of whiskey on his breath. "You've been drinking."

His face grows more serious, and his eyes trail toward the men's room. "Hey, I've been trying to reach you. I think we should talk. Things have been left unfinished." He glances at my phone. "You've blocked me." He pauses. "From everything."

"Dom, I have nothing else to say. We don't need closure," I say. "You determined our closure when you slept with Maddie." Saying the words out loud makes me sick to my stomach.

"What the fuck? Why won't you let that go?" His eyes blaze into mine. "You need to let me explain what happened."

"We've been over this," I say, trying to keep my voice steady. But deep down, guilt gnaws at me for having moved on from him so quickly. But I didn't have a choice, he was one hundred percent toxic. But I can see the pain etched onto his face, and it tugs at my heartstrings.

Just as I'm about to cave and listen to him more, Lucas's shadow fills the space behind me, his face darkening when he sees Dom's hand reach for my waist.

"Get your hands off her," he growls, his protective instincts kicking in.

"Lucas, it's okay," I try to intervene, but Dom cuts me off.

"Who the hell do you think you are?" he sneers, addressing Lucas. "Her boss, right?" He turns his attention back to me, shock in his eyes. "What, you're sleeping with him now?"

"Watch your mouth," Lucas warns, grabbing Dom by the shoulders and practically launching him toward the door. "Stay away from her," he adds, his voice steely, blocking Dom's access to me.

Dom peers back at me, lips pressed together like it's far from over, and then he turns, shoulders slumped, and leaves. I turn in the direction of where he came from and see two of his friends at a high table, staring at Lucas with dropped jaws.

I swallow hard, my mind still reeling from the sudden confrontation. Lucas's fierce protectiveness sends a thrill down my spine, but at the same time, I feel a pang of guilt for the hurt expression on Dom's face as he was thrown out of the bar.

And then his friends, they kept their heads down, nursing their beers, probably praying Lucas wouldn't make a move at them.

My eyes trailed back to Lucas, taking in his muscular frame, stern expression, and bulging biceps. No wonder none of them stood up to him; he's terrifying. But then his hand moves around my waist, and he leans in to whisper in my ear, turning my knees to jelly.

"Are you okay?" he asks.

"Yes," I exhale, trying to shake off the guilt and confusion. "Just wasn't expecting to see him."

He nods. "I think he might keep his distance from here forward."

I smile. "Yeah, something tells me you're probably right."

He flags the barman over and orders a Jameson, knocking it back with ease, the dark liquid disappearing without so much as a wince. "Let's forget about him and enjoy our celebration, alright?" Lucas suggests, his eyes softening as he takes my hand.

"Alright," I agree, heart still pounding.

He leans in close again. "I think I've had enough pub excitement for one day." He rubs his temples. "I'd really like it if you could come home with me tonight."

My heart races at the thought, but then reality sets in. "Lucas, I really want to," I say, unable to hide the desire in my voice. "But I promised Chloe I'd go dress shopping with her tonight." My face shows the deep disappointment I feel.

"Damn," he sighs. "Well, how about we explore *my* neighborhood next time? It's my turn to show *you* around."

"Yeah, I'd like that." Relief washes over me as I see the disappointment in his eyes replaced by a hint of excitement. "Just promise me you'll stay in touch tonight, alright? I need to know you're okay after everything that's happened today."

"Emily," he chuffs, a small grin tugging at his lips. "I can handle a minor run-in with an ex-boyfriend."

"Still," I insist, playfully swatting his arm.

"Alright, alright," he concedes, raising his hands in mock surrender. "I promise I'll keep in touch."

"Good," I say, satisfied, and I wrap my arms around him for a quick hug. His strong arms envelop me, and for a moment, we linger in each other's embrace.

We head out the door and our eyes lock, and for a moment, I feel as though time has stopped. The sounds of the city—honking cars, chattering passersby, and distant laughter—fade into the background, leaving only the steady rhythm of my heart pounding in my ears.

I glance at my vibrating phone and see Chloe's name light up. "Sounds like we might break some more rules," I whisper, feeling both exhilarated and terrified by the promise that hangs between us.

"Agreed," he murmurs as we walk back toward the gym, hand in hand.

# Chapter Ten (Lucas)

I watch from my spot on the sidelines as my fighters squeeze in their final practice before the grand showcase. Sweat drips from their brows, their muscles flexing with each expertly executed move. I've molded them into champions, and I feel a swell of pride as I take in their progress.

But lurking beneath that pride lies an undercurrent of worry. The martial arts world isn't exactly a walk in the park. It's packed to the brim with rivals and underhanded business tactics. Keeping a step ahead of the competition and ensuring that Walker Enterprises doesn't crumble into chaos is like juggling knives. And then there are people like Emily, who push all my buttons while somehow cranking up my desire for her. They say opposites attract, and for us, it's like we're magnets on steroids.

As if my thoughts have conjured them, the gym door swings open, and Chloe and Emily whirl in, their laughter ricocheting off the walls. They're a hurricane of energy and giggles, and I find myself grinning despite the storm of worries swirling in my head.

"Lucas! You won't believe the calamity we found ourselves in today," Chloe says between giggles.

"I'm all ears," I reply.

"Emily and I were on a wedding mission, and we stumbled into this shop that sold nothing but novelty cake toppers...." Chloe's voice trails off as she spots the fighters behind me.

"Wow, you've got a small army of martial arts superheroes here," she says, her eyes wide with awe.

"Thanks, Chloe," I respond with a nod, a rush of pride washing over me. "They're burning the midnight oil for the upcoming showcase."

"Emily, you should consider martial arts," Chloe teases, giving her a playful elbow. "It could be a great stress-buster after dealing with his pushy clients." She rolls her eyes at me.

"Maybe," Emily murmurs, her eyes flitting to mine. I can't help but speculate what's going on in her mind, and the familiar heat that always simmers between us sparks to life.

"Anyway," Chloe says, sweeping the previous topic aside, "we were having such a blast today that I lost track of time." Clapping her hands together, she adds, "You should have seen the cakes too!"

"Really?" I respond, doing my best to sound interested while studying Emily's reaction out of the corner of my eye. She's got a smile pasted on, but there's a shadow in her eyes that screams *"I'd rather be anywhere else."* Wedding planning is probably the last thing she wants to do.

"*Yup*," Chloe barrels on, blissfully unaware of Emily's discomfort. "We tasted everything from a heavenly chocolate ganache to a zingy raspberry lemonade, and we still couldn't crown a champion."

"Sounds like you two had quite the adventure," I say, remaining positive. But on the inside, I'm frowning at Chloe's lack of tact. Why would she pull Emily into this level of wedding prep when it's as clear as day that her emotions are still raw?

"Emily, which did you like best?" Chloe asks, eyes wide.

"Um, well," Emily stammers, caught off guard by the question. "I guess I kind of liked the… the lavender-honey one? It was a bit out of the box, you know?"

"Ooh, yes!" Chloe nods vigorously. "That one was really unexpected. Maybe we'll pick that one."

As the chatter rolls on, I sneak another look at Emily. Her smile is fragile and doesn't quite reach her eyes, sending a wave of protectiveness crashing over me. That's it; it's time to draw the line on Chloe's unwitting emotional tug-of-war with Emily.

"Chloe, why don't we give Emily a breather from all the wedding buzz?" I suggest. "She could use a break, right?"

"Lucas, we're just having fun," Chloe protests, but her voice wavers slightly. "Right, Em?"

"Of course," she chimes in, but there's a glimmer of relief in her eyes as they meet mine.

"Chloe," I start, doing my best poker face. "I actually need her for the rest of the day, anyway. A bunch of business stuff just washed up, and her genius is the life raft I need."

"Really? Now?" Chloe squints, suspicion seeping into her expression like she's just caught us raiding the cookie jar.

I glance back at my fighters to demonstrate how full my hands are. "Yep," I fib smoothly, slapping on a carefree smirk.

Emily sends me a look that's pure gratitude, her shoulders dropping. As much as I cherish Chloe, I can't shake the feeling that she's inadvertently putting Emily through a wringer with all this wedding hoopla, maybe even more so to keep us apart.

"Fine," Chloe grumbles, crossing her arms in a huff. "But don't overwork her. We've got a mountain of things to still do."

"Don't sweat it," I assure her. "We'll wrap things up and have Emily back to you before long."

Once Chloe finally leaves, I turn to Emily, who's now exhaling with what looks like a mix of relief and intrigue.

"Thank you," she whispers, a genuine smile on her lips.

"No problem." I shrug. "I couldn't bear to see you endure another cake war."

We share a chuckle, and I'm hit with a thunderbolt of how stunning she is when she's free of worry. But there's something else nagging at my brain—something that's been gnawing at me since I caught Chloe's reaction to my needing Emily for the afternoon.

"Hey, Em," I say cautiously. "Isn't it kinda weird how Chloe seems to be pulling on you, like trying to take your time from me? It's almost like she doesn't want to share you anymore."

"Hm, maybe," she responds, her eyes narrowing as she thinks. "She has been kind of intense recently. Like acting surprised when I'm spending time here." She lifts her shoulders and smirks. "Plus, it was her idea from the start."

"Exactly," I agree. "Although, it was kind of our own idea at the very beginning, which is pretty cool." I lift my brows thinking of our first night together. "But when she matched us as business partners, I just don't think she expected... this." My finger points to her, then to me.

#

As the last echoes of grunts and punches against bags bounce off the gym walls, and the fighters cool down on the mats, Emily and I watch the after-workout scene. Our day has been busy, and a strong sense of accomplishment is in the air. We made more moves toward the Dubai deal and were just waiting now for a formal response. Seemed like a perfect time to take a detour from the daily grind of the gym.

"Come on," I say, nudging into Emily, gesturing my head towards the gym's exit. "Wanna get out of here? No sense in just waiting around. Dubai could take days to review the offer. Would be a shame to waste the rest of the afternoon." I shrug innocently. "My turn to show you around *my* neighborhood."

Her eyes light up. "Okay," she replies with a grin. "I'm curious to see your part of town," she says, as we step into the cool Boston air.

We hop into my SUV and leave the dojo behind us, as I bomb down Clarendon Street toward Back Bay.

"Okay," she nods. "Not too far from Southie. Same side of the city anyway. We're practically neighbors." She smiled brightly.

Pulling into a private parking garage, we leave the SUV and head down Arlington, along the edge of the Public Garden, while I make no mention that we're passing my building. I don't want her to get the wrong impression, thinking I want to take her home with me. Though, she wouldn't be altogether wrong.

Instead, we walk through the theater district, and I point out the various theaters and well-known performance spaces, feeling like a tour guide. For some reason, it's my favorite part of the city and I want to walk through it with Emily.

"I love this spot," she says. "Have you been to any performances here?" Her gaze sweeps over the ornate facades and flashing signs of the historic buildings.

"Never by my own choosing," I reply with a chuckle, stopping at a coffee cart. "But once inside, I have to admit, I don't hate it."

Emily hums, appearing somewhat impressed. We grab two hot coffees, the best in town from a small vendor who knows his stuff, and as we get ready to move again, I notice the prolonged glances from assholes in suits checking her out. I can't blame them, the way her jeans fit so perfectly and her gorgeous blonde hair blowing across her shoulders. My chest inflates at first, feeling jealousy rising, but then I decide instead to feel lucky to have her with me.

"Hey, Em, you're causing some serious whiplash," I tease, giving her a playful elbow nudge.

"Really? And what about you, Mr. Navy SEAL Jujitsu Master?" she retorts. "You're quite a spectacle too, you know."

"Can't dispute that." I grin.

#

We weave through the crowd of people on Newbury Street, dodging a group of tourists and a street musician strumming Bob Marley. The shops and restaurants line the street for blocks, their windows spilling out every luxury item possible. Emily beams with enthusiasm as she bounces from store window to store window, her eyes twinkling.

I gaze up at Rebecca's, the iconic bistro that sits on the corner of Newbury and Boylston, and my stomach grumbles. "Hey, how about we snag some grub from here? We can take it back to my place," I propose, motioning toward the café.

She nods, her mesmerizing green eyes sparkling with mischief.

We step inside and are immediately hit with a blast of warm air carrying scents of garlic and rosemary. The space is cozy and inviting, with muted lights and rows of booths lining the walls. As we wait for our order, I can feel the tranquility in the air; it's like we're in our own little world.

Once everything's all packed up neatly, I look over at her expectantly. "Ready to roll?" I ask, my hand instinctively gravitating toward hers.

She smiles at me knowingly as she curls her fingers around mine. "Yes, sir," she responds before tugging me out of the restaurant and into the night.

We weave our way to the end of Newbury Street, past fluttering streetlights, until we finally reach my building. I can practically hear the gears in her head grinding in curiosity as we approach the entrance.

"This is your bat cave?" she asks, her eyebrows lifting.

"Affirmative," I shoot back, nonchalantly.

The doorman stands tall at his post and tips his hat as he opens the heavy glass door to let us inside. Emily gasps, her jaw dropping open at the sight of the sprawling lobby. Sparkling chandeliers hang from the ceiling, casting an ethereal glow over everything. The marble floors shine like mirrors, and you can almost feel the energy radiating off them.

"Holy shit, Lucas," she murmurs, her eyes wide with wonderment.

I shrug nonchalantly and say, "Ah, it's just a little something I picked up." I don't want her to think that I'm just flashing my cash.

As we step into the elevator, I feel her hand trembling slightly in mine. I turn to look at her and see a familiar twinkle in her eyes that only appears when she's really excited. We ride up the express route, the anticipation growing with every floor that passes. The elevator doors slide open, and Emily gasps at the sight before us—my penthouse, its walls of windows giving an impressive view of the Common below.

"Lucas, this is... wow," she breathes.

I smile as I watch her wander around the living room, her slender fingers tracing along the leather sofa and lingering on each piece of artwork that hangs on the walls.

"Welcome to my humble abode."

She shakes her head in disbelief, scanning the room once more before gasping. "Is that a grappling mat?" she exclaims, pointing to the far side of the sunken living area.

I chuckle. "Guilty as charged. I guess I can never really leave my martial arts behind."

She teases me with a playful tilt of her head. "Care to give me a quick lesson?"

I smirk back at her. "Are you sure? I wouldn't want to hurt you, now," I tease.

"Come on, tough guy. Show me what you've got," she goads, stepping onto the mat and assuming a mock fighting stance.

I can't resist the challenge in her eyes, so I step onto the mat with her. Our bodies move together in a tangle of limbs as we start with some basic wrestling moves. The intensity grows between us until it seems like sparks are flying off our skin. We're both breathing hard when she finally concedes defeat, her hands weakly gripping my shoulders as I pin her down. Our eyes meet and all traces of laughter evaporate, replaced by an undeniable desire that neither of us can ignore.

"Emily...," I whisper, my voice gravelly with a yearning I can't hide. She surges up, claiming my lips with hers, our mouths moving together as if they were always meant to.

Our hands move urgently, tugging off our clothes as we stumble down the hallway toward my bedroom. Our bodies crash through the door, and we fall onto the bed. It feels like an oasis beneath us, and I've never been more aware of the contrasts between Emily's soft skin and the masculine design of my room. It's as if she's brought a missing piece of myself into my life, a balance I didn't know I needed until now.

I pull her close, my heart thundering as we kiss with urgency. Her body is electric beneath me, and I want to devour her entirely. My hands move all over her, exploring the curves of her body while she moves her fingers along my chest.

We pull away and I look into her eyes, blazing with a passion that thrills and terrifies me.

"Emily," I whisper, my fingertips tracing the curve of her cheek. "You have no idea what you do to me."

"Show me," she murmurs, her voice low and sultry.

Our lips meet again, and this time there is a newfound intimacy in our touch. I feel my heart swell as I hold her close, feeling the warmth of her breath on my skin and realizing a ravenous part of myself I'd never known existed.

"I want you so bad," I breathe, my voice husky with desire.

I stand up beside the bed, looking down at her with smoldering eyes.

I grab her off the bed, my fingers grazing the zipper of her jeans. She stops me, and I watch as she slips out of her remaining bits of clothing, standing just in her lace panties. My eyes trail along her body and she watches me, unafraid.

Kicking off my pants, I pull her close and kiss her again in an embrace filled with desire and passion. We move back to the bed, lying together entwined in each other's arms. As I kiss the sensitive skin along her neck, she gasps my name. In response, I whisper, "Tell me what you want."

"Make love to me," she breathes.

In this moment, I know exactly how to make her feel alive.

My hands move lower, cupping her breasts, and my thumbs rub her nipples as they harden. I can feel her back arching with anticipation as I explore her. I kiss her lips, then move to her neck, and then to her breast, where I suck on her nipple, feeling the wave of pleasure ripple through her body as she lets out a moan. Hooking a finger around the lace of her panties, I pull them off her and move down between her legs, kissing a trail lower and lower until my tongue finds its way to the most sensitive part of her. I push her legs open wider, seeing every part of her, and nearly explode.

I tease and lick her hot flesh, pushing her closer and closer to the edge with each stroke as she lifts her hips and moans in pleasure. Teetering on the brink of bliss, I want nothing more than to join her in this moment. So, I rise and hover over her, kissing her neck softly.

"You're so beautiful," I pant. "I want you more than anything."

And as she lifts herself to me, wrapping her legs around my hips, I push myself inside of her slowly and she gasps, driving me wild. With each thrust becoming increasingly urgent, our bodies move together in perfect sync with desire threatening to consume us. My hands move up to caress her face as our heavy breathing fills the air. This is what it means to be alive.

I lick my fingers and slide them down between her legs. I feel the energy radiating from her as she quivers in anticipation. I tease and flick her sensitive spot, pushing her higher and higher with each thrust until she finally erupts in gasps of pleasure.

Her body trembles as I follow, calling out her name before letting out one last gasp of blissful satisfaction. We stay entangled for a few moments as we recover our breath, then I kiss her tenderly before rolling over and wrapping my arm around her body.

"You're incredible," I whisper in her ear. "Stay with me tonight."

# Chapter Eleven (Emily)

I blink my eyes open, the soft morning light filtering through the floor-to-ceiling windows of Lucas's bedroom. My heart pounds in my chest as I remember our passionate night together. He was the perfect lover, treating me like I was so special and taking care of me in every way. But then uncertainty creeps in like a thief. I wonder if he wants me to stay or if I should just slip out.

I cast a glance towards his mahogany dresser, my eyes instantly drawn to the scattered remnants of our late-night feast from Rebecca's Bistro. Crumpled napkins and empty wine glasses hold the evidence of our messy enjoyment, making me smile. It was the best nightcap for the activities that had distracted our hunger, proving we were ravenous for each other instead.

I can't help but feel vulnerable now, though, knowing how closed-off he can be, and knowing our loyalty to Chloe. I carefully slide out of bed and pull on my jeans, trying not to disturb him. There's just no way I could handle a cold shoulder or any sign of regret from him.

As if he possesses some uncanny intuition, his eyes suddenly blink open, piercing through the dimness of the room.

"Where do you think you're going?" he says with a sleepy drawl, his eyebrow arching in amusement.

"Uh, I was just...." Caught off guard, I stammer, searching for words.

"Trying to sneak away from me?" He raises an eyebrow, amused. "Get back here." His arm opens invitingly, encouraging me into the comfort of his bed.

Not one to argue with a former Navy SEAL and having learned my lesson on the mat in his living room, I obey and crawl back into bed. He pulls me close and plants a lingering kiss on my lips—his way of making it clear that he wants me to stay. My heart swells as relief washes over me.

"Let's make breakfast," he suggests, a playful glint in his eyes. "I've been told my omelet skills are lethal."

A grin unfurls across my face. "Sounds perfect," I say, elated by the prospect of having more time to savor with him.

We head to his massive kitchen, complete with marble countertops, shiny stainless-steel appliances, and enough gadgetry to make even Iron Man jealous. As we chop vegetables and whisk eggs, our laughter fills the air, making the space feel warm and inviting.

"Actually," I say, pausing for a moment, "I know we have contracts to draw up, but instead of going straight to the gym, I need to swing by the shelter first, to drop off some papers." I force a smile, my teeth peeking through my lips, hoping to alleviate any stress my detour might cause.

"That's fine," he murmurs, focused on his cast-iron pan as it heats up on the gas stove. "I need to get a workout in anyway." He adds butter to the pan, then looks up. "Or I could go with you." His eyebrows lift in silent question.

I smile, continuing to shred a block of cheddar, while inside, a swarm of butterflies takes flight, but I hope my exterior remains composed. "Yeah, that sounds perfect."

After the best omelet of my life, we clean up the kitchen and head out the door, leaving his sun-filled penthouse behind us. As the elevator doors slide open, the doorman sees us and smirks, pushing open the large wooden door of the building, leading us onto the bustling sidewalk of Newbury Street.

A short walk and we find his SUV in the parking garage where we'd left it the day before, and I realize now how close we were to his apartment at that time. We likely walked right past it as we made our way to the theater district. I shook my head, replaying every event from the day before, each moment better than the last.

Bombing down Berkeley, feeling like a celebrity in his high-end vehicle, blacked out windows and rims that cause people to look twice, I glance over at him, noticing the muscles running up his arm from his grip on the wheel. He appears so unapproachable to most, tall, strong, ruggedly handsome, but to me, I seem to already understand who he truly is... and I like it.

"So, what made you agree to take a detour to the shelter," I ask, brows lifted.

He shrugs. "I wouldn't mind seeing Charlie again," he says, a hint of fondness creeping into his voice, then glances at me. "And it seemed like a better idea than the two of us getting stuck in the grind at the gym. More time to relax." His words hang in the air between us, sharing the understanding of wanting more time together.

I find myself nodding in agreement, fully aware that our casual demeanor would be shockingly replaced with professionalism once we set foot in the gym, as always.

After navigating a few more winding turns, the familiar sign of the shelter comes into view, the rich, cobalt blue letters popping against the faded sun-bleached wood. As we enter the building, I find myself drawn to the counter to talk with Jayne, and Lucas wastes no time and makes a beeline for Charlie's cage.

"So, these are the tax documents you'll need when you file," I say, handing the forms to Jayne. "The tax-exempt number is here." I point, but my words trail off as I notice Jayne isn't paying attention. Her gaze is transfixed on Lucas and Charlie, watching their interactions.

"That's just about the cutest thing I've ever seen," she gushes. "The dog, I mean." She laughs, nudging me. "No, but in all seriousness, those two were made for each other."

Her words echo with my sentiments, thoughts I've been having since the moment Lucas and Charlie first met. But I just wasn't sure if Lucas was ready to take on the reality of dog ownership yet.

"Hm," I muse aloud, considering a way to help deepen their bond. "Maybe I'll see if he wants to take Charlie for a walk." I tip my head, knowing it will only bring them closer.

Before I even fully commit to the idea, Jayne, ever the intuitive soul, hands me the leash, and I flash a mischievous smile.

Approaching Lucas, I listen as he speaks soothing words to Charlie, and once I have the dog in my view, I see his eyes, usually a whirlpool of anxious energy, but now exuding serene tranquility as he stares at Lucas. It's a sight that sends a flutter of hope through my heart.

"Hey," I whisper. "Want to take him for a walk?" I hold out the leash, its worn leather handle swaying gently.

"We can do that?" he asks in surprise, his voice laced with a childlike excitement that makes me chuckle. "Absolutely."

With a swift, confident motion, he clicks the leash onto Charlie's collar, and we head out toward Peter's Park, enjoying the crisp morning air.

As we stroll, we pass by a weathered VFW Post, its worn bricks bearing the invisible marks of countless stories. Two elderly veterans, their age-worn uniforms lending them an air of humble dignity, are leaving the building, their camaraderie holding them together stronger than any physical force.

Lucas halts mid-stride and lifts his hand in a firm salute. The sudden gesture causes the veterans to stop their conversation midsentence and return the salute with matching solemnity. As I watch this silent exchange, chills run up my arms making my fine hairs stand on end. Then we all continue walking in our separate ways, the moment imprinted in my memory.

"Oh my God," I breathe, the impact of the scene still ricocheting in my chest. "That was so powerful." I stare at him in awe. "There's so much most people don't know about the things vets have been through, the bonds they share."

He slows and pats Charlie's head. "You're right. Very few civilians think about it—ever." His gaze is distant as if lost in a memory. "And I guess that comfortable complacency is part of what we protect, part of freedom."

His words linger in the air, a stark reminder of the sacrifices of those who serve. I exhale deeply, speechless at what goes on in the military, grateful for the ability to walk around this beautiful city safely and freely.

"It's the haunting part that they don't warn us about, though. The part that follows us when we return to civilian life." Lucas's hand continues to stroke Charlie's fur. He holds the dog's gaze and the two of them are content in the space between them. "Only those who have worn the uniform can fully understand that part."

I nod in quiet acknowledgment, acutely aware of the internal battles he fights, the nightmares that refuse to let him rest, the PTSD that's always an uninvited guest.

"And it's always the least expected event that replays, like a broken record in the mind, over and over." His voice is twinged with weary resignation.

"Is there one that repeats for you?" I gently probe, wanting to understand the labyrinth of his thoughts better.

He hesitates as if weighing the costs of opening a sealed chapter, then says, "There was this one mission," he begins, his gaze never leaving Charlie. "We were tasked with rescuing a group of hostages from a heavily guarded compound. But when we got there, we realized it was rigged with explosives, a ticking time bomb ready to wipe out every soul inside. If we didn't act fast, everyone would be killed."

I listen without interruption, giving him space.

"Ultimately, I was the one to make the call, to disarm the bombs and extract the hostages, knowing full well it put my team at risk." His voice is steady, but I can sense the pain lurking beneath the surface. "I deployed my bomb crew, young guys, brilliant minds, and watched two of them blow to bits right in front of my eyes." His words falter for a moment, his silence punctuating the echoes of his past, and he clears his throat. "It's a scene that refuses to fade."

As I listen to the rawness of his confession, deep sadness builds in my gut, knowing he was scarred, always doubting if a different decision may have ended better.

"You have to remember the faces of the people who were saved that day," I whisper. "The sacrifices of the soldiers from your platoon, they were the lifeline for everyone else. Their bravery made survival possible." I reached my arms around his ribs. "War is a horrible thing. None of it was caused by you."

I know my words are only that, mere words, but I feel his taut muscles gradually relax under my hold and I'm reassured that I can help, even in this small way.

And then my thoughts drift to my wounds, Dom's infidelity, and the callous disregard with which he discarded me. A stark realization dawns on me that Lucas, despite his haunted past, would never want to hurt me in that way, he'd never want to hurt anyone. He just needs peace.

As we stroll into the park, I notice how the sunlight filters through the trees, casting warm golden rays onto the ground. The world suddenly seems brighter, filled with possibilities. I glance over at Lucas, who appears lost in thought, his brow furrowed. Instinctively, I reach out and give his hand a reassuring squeeze.

"Hey, everything's good," I whisper, offering him a small, encouraging smile, and he squeezes my hand back.

Suddenly, Charlie catches sight of another dog approaching in the distance. He slows down, lowers his head, and evaluates the potential threat. I can't help but laugh as I watch him, struck by the similarity between Charlie's reaction and Lucas's protective instincts.

But then I notice Lucas, his spine straightened, eyes sharp, as he feeds off Charlie's energy.

"Look at that," I interrupt the mounting tension. "Charlie's channeling his inner Navy SEAL!"

Lucas's shoulders immediately drop, as he realizes there's not a true threat. "Looks like he's taking his cues from me," he says with a grin. He then leans down and speaks soothingly to Charlie, letting him know there's no reason to be on high alert. "It's okay, buddy. There's no threat here. Just another friendly dog."

As we continue our walk, I practically see the anxiety washing off Lucas as he keeps stride with Charlie. I can see the two together and wonder if Lucas would be able to take on the challenge of having a dog. The two of them need each other.

Casting a sidelong glance at him, I open my mouth to voice my thoughts, but he beats me to it. His grip on the leash tightens, his knuckles white against the dark leather, as he draws in a deep breath.

"I wonder...." His voice is slightly hesitant. "I wonder if I should consider adopting Charlie."

# Chapter Twelve
## (Lucas)

Time is closing in before the championship fight and everything in my life takes a back burner. I can't focus on anything except getting my fighters ready. Every detail must be perfect in order to continue Walker Enterprise's climb in the world of MMA.

"Pick up the pace, team! We need more power, more speed!" My words echo around the gym, bouncing off the sweat-streaked mats and tension-filled air. This showcase is a big deal, a game-changer, and no one needs an extra memo to understand that.

The gym is bustling with activity, every fighter in the room delivering punch after punch, sharp kicks slicing through the air. Their muscles flex with exertion, their focus riveting. My gaze scans the room, taking in each fighter, scrutinizing every move. My brain is a hurricane of tactics and techniques, constantly analyzing, revising, and improving.

"Damien, guard up!" My voice cuts through the chaos as I stride over to one of my top fighters, currently choke-holding another ace. "You're an open book right now."

"Got it, Coach," Damien pants, his face covered with determination and sweat as he tweaks his stance.

There's a tangible tension in the air, yet underlying it all is a bond of brotherhood among the fighters. They know I've got their backs, and the trust they place in me is absolute. The mounting stress, though, starts to nibble at the corners of my patience.

"Break time, five minutes," I order, rubbing the back of my neck. The fighters collapse onto the mat, gulping down water and wiping sweat off their faces. I watch them, doing my best to suppress the anxiety brewing inside me. "Keep in mind," I call out again, "we're a team. One man down, we're all down. Let's make every move count.

"Lucas," a voice sneers from the doorway. A chill runs down my spine as I recognize the malicious tone. My muscles tense immediately, ready for a fight.

"Carlo," I greet through gritted teeth, turning to face him. "What do you want?"

"Nothing much," he replies nonchalantly, sauntering into the gym. "Just thought I'd drop by and lend you some advice." He smirks, eyeing my fighters. "Seems like you could use it."

"Your 'advice' is neither needed nor wanted," I snap back, crossing my arms.

"Suit yourself." He shrugs, feigning innocence. "But if I were you, I'd work on their defense." He points at one of my fighters, who is visibly annoyed but remains silent.

"Get out," I order, barely keeping my anger in check.

"Fine, fine," he says, raising his hands in mock surrender. "Just remember, Lucas, my offer stands. Your fighters are always welcome at my gym." He flashes a devious grin that makes my blood boil.

"Your gym?" I scoff. "You mean the place where you breed cheaters and addicts? No thanks. We have standards here."

"Ouch." He feigns hurt, placing a hand over his heart. "You really know how to hit where it hurts."

"Speaking of hitting," I retort, "maybe you should focus on teaching your fighters not to intentionally injure their opponents."

"Low blow, Lucas," Carlo snaps back, his eyes narrowing. "At least my fighters aren't caught up in sexual assault scandals."

"Those accusations were proven false," I growl, clenching my fists.

Carlo smirks, clearly enjoying getting under my skin. "Well, if you're so confident in your coaching, maybe you won't mind a little competition for the Dubai showcase."

"Bring it on," I challenge, my eyes locking on to his. "But don't be surprised when my fighters wipe the floor with yours."

"Careful, Lucas," he taunts as he backs toward the door. "Pride goes before a fall."

"Get out," I snarl, my patience wearing thin.

"Alright, alright," he concedes, holding his hands up. "I'll leave you to your... training." He spits the last word like it's an insult but makes no moves toward the exit.

Just as I'm about to physically remove this arrogant prick from my gym, the door flies open, and Chloe bursts in, her eyes wild with panic.

"Lucas! Thank God you're here!" she exclaims, almost out of breath. "You have to help me! Mom's gone off the deep end and is making the most irrational demands!"

"Chloe, now's not a good time—" I snarl through my teeth, glancing back at Carlo, who's smirking at the interruption, trying to listen in.

"Lucas, please, this is important! I need your help, or this wedding is going to be a disaster!"

"Fine," I grit out, turning back to Carlo. "Leave. Now."

"Alright, alright," he says with a grin, sauntering toward the door. "Good luck with your personal drama. I'm sure Miss Emily will be interested to hear you have a sidepiece." He watches Chloe's reaction. "Aw, come on, Lucas," Carlo taunts, a malicious grin spreading across his face. "I mean, it's pretty ballsy to be fucking your contract negotiator while keeping a sweet little thing like this around."

Carlo's gloating grin fuels the fire in me, and I can't take it any longer. I lunge toward him, fists clenched, ready to wipe that smug look off his face. But just as my punch is about to connect with his jaw, my fighters grab me by the arms, pulling me back with surprising strength.

"Lucas, man, he ain't worth it!" one of them shouts, trying to reason with me even as I struggle against their hold.

"Get him out of here," I growl through gritted teeth, and two of my fighters nod in agreement. With a mix of determination and assertiveness, they move Carlo to the door, tossing him out without a second thought.

"Stay away from our gym!" one of them yells after him. The door slams shut, finally putting an end to Carlo's toxic presence—for now, at least.

My heart is pounding in my chest, and I force myself to take deep, slow breaths, using the techniques Emily taught me to regain control over my emotions. As much as I want to chase after Carlo and pound him into the ground, I know I need to get myself together. So, I quickly make my way to my office, hoping for a moment to clear my head.

But as I push open the door, I realize that privacy is too much to ask for right now. Chloe followed me into the office, her eyes still filled with hurt and disbelief from Carlo's comment about Emily.

"Chloe, please," I plead, my voice cracking, "just let me explain."

"Explain?" she scoffs, crossing her arms defensively. "You really think there's anything you can say that'll make this okay?"

"Look, I know this isn't what you wanted," I admit, running a hand over my hair in frustration. "But what happened between Emily and me... it wasn't planned. It just... happened." I search her face for any sign of understanding, but she remains stoic.

"Lucas, you betrayed me," she says quietly. "You knew how important it was to me to keep things professional between you two, especially with everything going on, and you chose to ignore that."

"It's not betrayal—" I start, but she cuts me off with a shake of her head.

"Save it, Lucas. Just... save it." She drops down on my couch. "Especially when my wedding is right around the corner," she adds, her voice quivering. "Now I don't even know how to feel about Emily either."

"Emily would never mean to hurt you," I say, clenching my fists at my sides as I struggle to remain calm. "This isn't about you."

"Not about me? How you managed to destroy not only our friendship but also my entire wedding?" she demands, her face flushed with anger.

Her excessive level of drama is enough to push me over the edge, and I feel the pressure in my head rising, my neck and cheeks burning.

Just as I'm about to respond, the door swings open and Emily strides into the office, her eyes wide with concern. She takes in the scene before her, clearly aware that something has gone horribly wrong. Her gaze meets mine, and for a brief moment, we share an unspoken understanding of the gravity of the situation.

"Chloe," Emily says softly, stepping forward with an imploring look on her face. "I've been meaning to tell you. I was just trying to find the right time."

"Don't," Chloe warns, holding up a hand to stop her from approaching. "Right now, I don't think there's anything you can say that will make this better."

"Please," Emily pleads, desperation lacing her voice. "We never meant to hurt you. It wasn't planned. It just happened, and we didn't know how to tell you."

"Didn't know how to tell me?" Chloe scoffs, her eyes blazing. "Or didn't care enough to?"

"Chloe—" Emily starts, but I can't help cutting in.

"This isn't on Emily," I say firmly, unable to let her take the brunt of the blame. "It's on me, and I'll do whatever it takes to fix it."

"Fix it?" Chloe repeats, her voice dripping with disbelief. "I don't need a fix, Lucas. I need my brother and my best friend back."

# Chapter Thirteen
## (Emily)

I sit across from Chloe at our favorite Italian restaurant, the warm glow of the chandeliers casting a comforting light over our table. The twist in my gut makes it difficult to eat my pasta, as the thick tension from our altercation at the gym the other day overshadows the cozy ambiance. The dimly lit restaurant bustles with laughter and clinking glasses, but my thoughts are far from relaxed.

"Well, I'm glad you were willing to come out with me," I say, attempting to break down the wall between us.

Chloe takes a deep breath. "So, I guess we should just cut to the chase, right?" she replies, reaching for her glass of rosé. "About our fight at the gym...."

I wince inwardly, knowing this conversation is inevitable. With a deep breath, I brace myself for the discussion ahead. "Yeah, I know. That was... very unexpected. I'm sorry it happened like that."

She presses her lips together. "Emily, why didn't you tell me about you and Lucas?" she asks, her eyes narrowed.

My stomach clenches as I recall the moment I walked into Lucas's office and saw Chloe, the look on her face revealing all. "I know. I'm sorry I didn't tell you sooner. It was unexpected and we didn't want to upset you. It's just... complicated."

"Complicated?" She raises an eyebrow. "You're fucking my brother, Emily. That doesn't just make it complicated; it makes it forbidden. Isn't that breaking girl code?"

I roll my eyes, trying to lighten the mood. "My best friend's brother? It's kind of a thing, isn't it?" I shake my head when I see she's not having it. "Look, I never expected to meet someone like Lucas. I literally fell for him before I even knew he was your brother."

"But then you found out who he was. You should have backed off then." She sits back in her chair with a huff. "It's like, too close to family, you know? It's icky."

"Chloe, it's not like that. You're making it sound like incest or something." I take a deep breath. "I hardly knew he even existed. You rarely mentioned him. Ever."

"That doesn't matter. Once you learned the truth, you should have known he was off-limits," she counters, a hint of jealousy in her voice. "I thought we were supposed to be best friends. And now you're sneaking around with my brother behind my back. It's just not right."

I look down at my plate, knowing she's right in a lot of ways, and guilt washes over me.

"It just... happened. We couldn't help how we felt about each other," I whisper. "I never meant to upset you."

"Whatever," she sighs, stabbing at her food. "But you have to admit, it's pretty messed up."

"Is it really that bad, though?" I ask. "Now that you know. Like, maybe it will bring us all closer."

"Maybe." She shrugs. "But it still feels like a betrayal."

Her words continue to sting, every one of them. "I never meant to hurt you," I say sincerely, reaching across the table to take her hand. "You're my best friend, and that will never change."

"Whatever you say," she mutters, rolling her eyes. "And with my wedding coming up, this little romance creates such a mess."

Her mention of the wedding throws me. Is that what this is about? Her big day getting messed up.

"This won't interfere with your wedding, Chloe. At all."

"It would have been so much easier if you were still with Dom," she mutters.

Her words cut me, and I don't know why she would bring him up. Ever.

"Please," I beg, reminded of my disastrous relationship with Dom, who cheated on me multiple times, manipulated me, and gaslighted me at every turn. "I don't even want to think about him."

"Still, at least he wasn't my brother," she says, her tone holding finality as she finishes the wine in her glass with a big gulp.

I look down, taking my lumps, wondering if I really deserve them.

She looks at me and her judgmental glare softens slightly. "I'm just protective of my brother," she admits, her voice lightening. "And I worry about what might happen if things between you two go south. You're both very important to me and I don't want everything to get all fucked up."

I nod, understanding a little better.

"Emily," she says, almost hesitantly, as the waiter fills our glasses again. Her eyes are serious, and I can tell this isn't going to be a lighthearted request. "I want you to make a pact with me."

"*Okayyy?*" I say cautiously, feeling my guard go up.

"Promise me that you won't let things go any further with Lucas," she begs, her voice barely more than a whisper. "Just... put things on hold until after the wedding, at least."

My heart clenches in my chest at her words, and I struggle to find the right response. I know how much she cares about her brother, but it's clear she's struggling to come to terms with the fact that he's moving forward with his life now, without her.

And although I understand her concerns, I'm not sure I can bring myself to agree to her request. Lucas and I have something special, and I don't want to let it slip away because of some misguided notion of family loyalty.

"Chloe, I—" I begin, but am interrupted by my phone buzzing loudly on the table. I glance down to see a text from an unknown number, and my brow furrows in confusion.

"Who is it?" Chloe asks, tone laced with annoyance from the distraction.

"I don't know," I admit, swiping my finger across the screen to read the message.

*Meet me for drinks Emmy.*

The hairs on the back of my neck raise, as a chill runs through me. Only one person calls me by that name. How did they even get my number?

"Let me see," Chloe says, reaching for my phone. As she reads the message, a curious smirk crosses her face. "Oh, shit. It's Dom."

"Dom," I repeat, my pulse quickening. "What the hell does he want? Why does he keep stalking me?"

"Maybe he wants to apologize," she suggests, the smirk still playing at the corners of her mouth. "Or maybe he's finally realized what a huge mistake he made when he let you go."

"Chloe." I shake my head, trying to suppress the annoyance bubbling up inside me. "You know how toxic things were between me and Dom. Why would you even suggest that?"

"Maybe you should hear him out," she suggests, a little too casually for my liking. The fact that she's not more outraged on my behalf is disheartening.

"Really?" I ask, my voice betraying my disappointment. "After everything he put me through, you think I should just give him the time of day?"

She shrugs nonchalantly, her eyes focused on her own phone. "I don't know, Em. Maybe he's changed."

"Or maybe he hasn't," I counter, feeling a flare of anger. "You saw what happened between us. You were there when he cheated, when he lied, when he tried to control me. And now you're acting like none of it even happened."

"Fine," she huffs. "Do whatever you want. I'm just saying that talking to him might give you some closure or something."

"Thanks for the support," I mutter sarcastically, my heart aching at the thought that my best friend isn't standing by my side.

"Fine, fine," she relents, raising her hands in surrender. "It was just a thought. But you should at least text him back."

"Fine," I agree, quickly tapping out a message. "There. Now can we please drop this whole Dom thing and get back to what matters?" I look at her with a worried gaze. "Can we just be friends again? I don't want this weird tension between us."

I take a deep swig of my wine to swallow down the unsettled feelings about Chloe's odd behavior. It's as if she's forgotten all about the terrible things Dom put me through, and all she cares about now is keeping me away from Lucas.

\#

We finish our dinner and make our way back to the car, the lingering tension between us making the darkness seem even more oppressive. As Chloe and I walk through the dimly lit parking lot, tension hangs heavy in the air between us. The flickering lampposts cast distorted shadows on the asphalt, making me feel even more unsettled than I already am. But it's not just the darkness that's getting to me—it's the uncertainty of where my friendship with Chloe now stands.

I prepare to break the ice, maybe something about our next wedding-planning adventure, anything to get her back to the Chloe I love.

"Emily, what the fuck?" Her face falls as her voice crackles with fear.

I whip around and see a group of dark, intimidating figures emerge from the shadows of an alleyway. My heart races as they approach us, their bodies bulky and imposing. One man steps forward, his smug grin giving him away immediately.

"Hey there, beautiful," Carlo coos, eyeing me up and down like I'm a piece of meat. "Fancy running into you here."

"Carlo," I say coolly, masking the unease crawling under my skin. "What do you want?"

"Can't a guy just say hello?" he replies, feigning innocence. But his eyes tell a different story—hungry and predatory.

"Emily, get in the car," Chloe urges, her hand shaking as she fumbles with the keys. Judging from her last run-in with him at the gym, she knows his intentions are bad.

"Aw, don't be like that," Carlo drawls, stepping closer to me. His breath reeks of alcohol and cheap cologne. He glances at Chloe. "And look it here. The two of Lucas's mistresses, together. How unusual. Ménage à trois?" He licks his lips. "You'd have more fun with us, I swear."

My stomach churns at his insinuation, but I refuse to let him see how much he's getting to me. Instead, I focus on Lucas—his strong arms wrapped around me, his unwavering dedication to everything he holds dear. A surge of defiance fills me, and I muster up the courage to stand my ground.

"Thanks for the offer," I say through gritted teeth, "but I'd rather walk through a pit of fire."

"Your loss," Carlo shrugs, but his eyes narrow with annoyance. He lets out a sinister laugh.

"Emily!" Chloe calls out again, her voice trembling. She's managed to unlock the car, and she's waving me towards it.

Carlo's laughter dies down as his expression turns cold, his eyes boring into mine. "Lucas isn't what you think, sweetheart. He's crazy. Can't hold his shit." He spits onto the pavement. "You deserve a real man."

My blood boils from his trash talk, knowing Lucas is a million times a better man than Carlo. My hands clench into fists, every fiber of my being urging me to lash out at this arrogant fool.

"Lucas may be many things," I say, my voice steady but ice cold, "but he's not crazy. He's a master at his craft and is at the top of his game. Be prepared to be left in the dust." I watch his brows furrow. "And don't forget, you're the one skulking around in dark alleys, trying to intimidate women. Who's the loser here?"

Chloe's eyes widen as she watches our exchange, her body stiff with tension. She looks like she's about to piss herself. I can't blame her for feeling scared, but I refuse to let Carlo's threats dictate my actions.

"You should watch your mouth," Carlo hisses, stepping closer, eyes narrowed. His thugs shift their weight, sizing up the situation.

Carlo studies me and I can see the cogs turning in his head, weighing up the potential consequences of pushing me further. He scoffs and steps back, waving a dismissive hand.

"Don't say I didn't warn you, princess," he says, voice dripping with disdain.

"Trust me," I reply, my tone matching his, "I won't lose any sleep over you."

Chloe finally unfreezes and rushes over, grabbing my arm and practically drags me toward the car, casting fearful glances at Carlo and his thugs as we leave them behind. As we pull out of the parking lot, my heart still races with adrenaline, but I feel a huge sense of pride in standing up to Carlo.

"Emily," Chloe blasts, her voice shaking, "what the fuck was that?"

She stares over at me in disbelief as we drive away from Lucas's biggest rival, still shaking his head, not knowing what hit him.

## Chapter Fourteen
## (Lucas)

The gym is filled with adrenaline and sweat, as training and planning for Dubai are in full swing. Taking Walker Enterprises to the world championship in Dubai is the next move in bringing new sponsorships, title-holding fighters, and insane financial growth. I don't take for granted for a second that Emily helped make it all possible, so it's clear to me that my future planning includes her.

I'm in the middle of training my fighters when my phone buzzes with a text from Chloe. She says her car's tire is making a weird squeaking sound, and since she's in the neighborhood, she wants me to help her. I sigh, but I can't deny that taking care of my little sister is part of the assignment, so I slip on my jacket and grab the gym's toolbox.

As I walk out into the parking lot, I see Chloe's car pulling up. She parks like she owns the place, blocking two perfectly good spots. Her sunglasses rest on her nose, giving her an air of entitlement as she steps out. She waves at me like I'm her personal mechanic or something.

"Lucas! Thank goodness," she exclaims, strutting over to me. "I don't know what I would have done without you."

"You do realize I have a gym full of fighters waiting for me right now, right?" I say, trying to keep the annoyance out of my voice.

"Of course, no problem, but this is important too. I mean, I can't drive around with a squeaky tire. It could be dangerous." She grins innocently.

I shake my head at her dramatics. "Alright, let's take a look."

I crouch down to examine the tire, feeling the annoyance brew inside me. I have fighters waiting for me, but here I am, playing mechanic for Chloe.

"Anyway," she starts, brushing off my obvious irritation. "I have something much more interesting to tell you."

"Really?" I ask, half listening as I inspect the brake pads. "What could be more interesting than this?"

"Carlo," she says, her voice becoming serious. "He cornered Emily in the restaurant parking lot last night when we were trying to leave. He had his thugs with him too. It was actually kind of scary."

My hands freeze, and I feel my blood start to boil. "What the fuck are you talking about?"

"Oh, I figured Emily would have told you," she murmurs.

"Told me what, Chloe?" My patience is wearing thin. "Why didn't' Emily tell me this?"

She shrugs, watching me closely. "I don't know. She handled it like a badass, though. Told him where to go, for sure."

"Damn it," I mutter under my breath, my protective instincts for Emily kicking into overdrive. "I swear if that bastard laid a hand on her—"

"Lucas," she interrupts, placing a hand on my shoulder. "Calm down. Emily's fine. I just thought you should know. Carlo is out for you."

My anger boils over, and I slam the wrench onto the pavement with a loud clang. "That son of a bitch!" I curse. "What did he say to her? That asshole clearly has a death wish."

Chloe's eyes widen at my reaction as if she didn't expect me to lose it like this. She hesitates for a moment before she starts to describe the confrontation. "Well, he basically tried to tell her that you were crazy, and she should go with him instead. He was pretty creepy about it, though."

Fury rises inside me as I think about what might have happened.

"I shouldn't have left her alone like that," I mutter to myself. "She's a target now. I have to remember that and keep her safe."

"Actually," Chloe says, a bit of arrogance in her tone, "Emily handled it like a boss. She didn't need any rescuing." She hesitated in thought. "If anything, it was me who needed saving." She let out a small laugh. "But seriously, Emily stood up to that guy as if she were just as strong as him. Basically, told him to fuck off in no uncertain terms."

I can see the envy in Chloe's eyes as she recounts the story, and I have to admit, I'm impressed too. Emily's always been strong-willed and independent but taking on someone as dangerous and sleazy as Carlo… takes a special kind of courage.

"Damn," I whisper under my breath, my anger momentarily subdued by my admiration for Emily. But then the fury comes roaring back, and I can't help but think about what could've happened if things had gone differently. "What if he'd hurt you two? What if he'd done something worse?" My fists clench involuntarily at the thought, my knuckles whitening, and I have to force myself to take a deep breath to regain some semblance of control.

"Well, I'm pretty sure Emily can handle herself," she says, trying to reassure me.

"I just can't figure out why she didn't tell me." I shake my head.

Chloe pulls her eyes away from mine, looking anywhere but at me. And as if I wasn't already anxious enough, she says, "Maybe she's hiding something."

My heart rate accelerates to near exploding as Chloe infers that Emily might be holding secrets from me.

"What the fuck is that supposed to mean?" I blast at her.

Chloe watches my temper escalate, concern etched on her face. "I just mean, maybe there's a reason she didn't tell you about it, Lucas," she says cautiously.

"What reason could she possibly have?" I demand.

"Well…." She hesitates for a moment before continuing, "Maybe Emily has some secrets she's not ready to share. She has her own life too, you know."

My eyes widen from her callous approach. "Secrets? What are you talking about?" My heart races as I try to understand what Chloe is hinting at.

"Dom," she blurts out as if saying his name is a confession in itself. "He's been texting her."

My blood runs cold at the mention of her ex—the one guy who seems to have some inexplicable hold over Emily. The jealousy that courses through me is almost painful, and I struggle to maintain my composure. "How do you know that?" I ask tersely.

"I saw his text last night at the restaurant," Chloe admits, her voice small. "I didn't mean to pry, but it just... happened."

My heart stops and everything goes out of focus. I know I can handle anything Carlo comes at me with, but Emily's ex? I have no idea where things stand with that.

I feel the jealousy and frustration boil inside me, mixing with possible betrayal. "Why would he be texting her?"

"Beats me." Chloe shrugs nonchalantly, though I can see the mischief dancing behind her eyes. "But maybe she's just a little distracted right now."

My head spins with all this new information, a toxic cocktail of emotions surging through me—anger, jealousy, hurt. I hate the thought of Emily keeping secrets from me, especially involving Dom. But at the same time, she faced down Carlo in my defense, proving her loyalty. My mind swirls with confusion making me dizzy.

I drop back down under the wheel of her car, grab my wrench, and yank out a piece of metal wedged between the brake pads. I toss it aside and stand up, brushing the dust off my knees.

"Thanks for telling me, Chloe," I say, gritting my teeth. "I'll... figure it out."

"Okay. Good luck, Lucas," she replies, patting me on the arm before getting in her car. "Thanks for the fix!"

I watch her drive away, her disastrous words echoing in my head.

"What the fuck is Emily doing talking to Dom?" I mutter under my breath, my jealousy flaring up once more.

I can't shake the feeling of unease settling over me, anger and frustration building to almost a breaking point. Returning to the gym, I make a beeline for the punching bags. My fists collide with the bag, each strike releasing a small part of the tension coiling inside me. I hop back and surge forward again, kicking the bag, over and over. The other fighters pause their workouts to watch my unrelenting assault on it.

"Damn, what's got Lucas so fired up?" I overhear someone mutter under their breath.

My mind races as I continue to pummel the bag, every punch and kick centered on Carlo and Dom, every thought centered on Emily. She's been keeping secrets from me—not just about Carlo, but about Dom too. Why? Is she trying to protect me, or is there something else going on?

As much as I want to believe in her, I can't help but feel like she's slipping away, leaving me grappling with the fear of losing her. My breaths come in ragged gasps, my heart pounding in my chest. I need to get out of here; I need space to think.

"Lucas, man," Xavier calls out cautiously, "you alright?"

I shoot him a curt nod, though it's clear neither of us is convinced by the gesture. Unable to control the emotional turmoil swirling inside me, I realize I need to get away from the gym—away from everyone.

"Xavier, you're in charge," I bark, not waiting for a response as I storm toward the exit. I need to clear my head and figure out what's going on with Emily and me before it's too late.

I grab my keys off my desk and make my way out, desperate for some time alone to process everything. My thoughts are a tangled mess, Emily's secrets and Dom's persisting presence in her life gnawing at me from the inside. I know I should give her space, but it's tearing me apart.

As I climb into my SUV, my phone buzzes with an incoming text. Glancing at the screen, my heart leaps for a moment as I see Emily's name.

I slide the phone back in my pocket and gun the engine, shooting gravel behind my wheels, as I bomb out of the lot.

## Chapter Fifteen
## (Emily)

I pace back and forth in my living room, biting my nails as I stare at my phone. Lucas wasn't answering my calls or texts and the silence was very unlike him. And now, with half the day gone by, I have no idea what's going on. I need to tell him about the whole Carlo thing from last night, particularly before anything else happens between them. My anxiety twists in my stomach, needing to process everything with him.

I tap out a message for Chloe, my fingers trembling. The last thing I want to do is get her involved, but maybe she knows something and can help.

I wait, watching the three dots on my phone as she texts me back. But then my heart jumps into my throat, seeing her cryptic message.

*Em, I think you should talk to him.*

I toss my phone down and search for my keys. I had to find Lucas and get answers, one way or another.

Driving to the gym, I review every interaction we had the previous day. Everything seemed to check out and it made no sense that he would be mad at me. Plus, ghosting someone when you're angry is not an option for me and I won't have it.

Finally, I pull into the lot, no memory of the drive there, and I barrel into the gym. The familiar scent of sweat and metal assaults my senses, heightening my concern. I scan the space for any sign of his tall, broad form, but no luck. He's nowhere to be seen.

My eyes land on Xavier, talking with another fighter on the mat. He notices me and raises an eyebrow in curiosity. As he directs the fighter into a new posture, he then walks toward me, his expression carefully neutral.

"Emily, what are you doing here?"

"Have you seen Lucas?" I ask, trying not to sound too desperate. "He's not answering my calls or texts."

He hesitates for a moment before replying, "He went home." He pauses, pressing his lips together. "Maybe you should go talk to him."

His words were like a punch to my gut. Chloe had said the same thing. Something was going on and I seemed to be the only one who had no clue.

With stealth focus, like nothing else in the world matters, I drive to his building, heart pounding. As I make my way to the door, I have no clue how I'll get inside and pray the doorman will know me.

I approach the door, the most convincing smile on my face, and it swings open with a warm welcome. I exhale for miles.

"Good day, Miss," the doorman says. "Here to see Mr. Walker?"

"Yes, thank you," I reply. "He's expecting me."

"Right, so," he gestures his arm to the elevator. "Up you go, then." And he smiles, turning back to the door.

As I ride the elevator up to Lucas's penthouse, anxiety knots my stomach tighter with every passing floor. I have no idea what I'll find or how he'll treat me and the unknown of it all is terrifying.

The elevator reaches the top floor and I punch in the code he used the last time, the same as the gym security code. As the doors slide open, I cross the threshold, and my footsteps echo softly against the cool, marble flooring. The apartment is full of light streaming in from the enormous windows, highlighting the empty furniture. An uncanny silence fills the air, giving me an unsettled feeling, but then I hear movement, subtle thuds, and music coming from farther within the penthouse.

"Lucas?" I call out cautiously, my heart pounding in my chest, as I move toward the living room. The sound of thumping music hits me as I walk deeper into the space.

And there, at the back, I see him on his mat, doing push-ups and sit-ups with a fierceness I've never seen before. His body is drenched in sweat, and his eyes are locked on the wall.

He doesn't respond, just continues his punishing workout as if I'm not even there.

"Lucas," I call out again, but still no response. I'm sure he can hear me. "Lucas, please," I beg, stepping closer to him. "Tell me what's going on?"

He finally stops and looks up at me, his eyes filled with pain and anger that sends shivers down my spine.

I rush to his side. "You're scaring me."

For a moment, he just lies there on the floor, breathing heavily from his push-ups. Then he rolls onto his back and sits up, avoiding my gaze.

"Emily," he says hoarsely. "What are you doing? Why are you here?" He wipes his head with his sweat rag. "I don't have time to be dicked around with."

I pull back in shock. "What?"

He exhales and glances at me. "I heard about your run-in with Carlo. Funny how it never occurred to you to maybe tell me that my nemesis assaulted you. I have to hear it from my sister?" He pauses. "The next day."

He stares at me unblinking as the blood drains from my head.

"That's what this is about? This is why you won't answer my calls?" I stare back. "What the fuck, Lucas?"

He remains silent.

"I was going to tell you this morning," I continued. "I didn't see a need to give you a sleepless night over it." I took a breath. "He didn't hurt me. It was just... uncomfortable." I glance down, realizing now that I should have told him right away.

His temper and his PTSD threw me off track. I was trying to protect him but stupidly did so with important information.

I kneel beside him, trying to catch his eye. "You're right. I should have told you last night," I say, watching him for a response. "I care about you, Lucas. I didn't want to upset you."

"Care about me?" He snorts, finally looking at me with a mix of disbelief and hurt. "Funny way of showing it."

His anger is still heightened, catching me off guard. For a long moment, he remains silent, making me wonder what's going on in his head.

He finally takes a deep breath and looks at me. "I need to know everything that happened with Carlo. Every detail."

I nod in agreement. "I know. I'll tell you everything."

He turns his head and gazes out the window. "I know about Dom too." He grabs his sweat rag, wipes his head with it again, and throws it at the wall.

My breath catches as my thoughts spiral. I race through my mind, trying to figure out what he could be talking about. The only interaction I'd had with Dom was....

"Why didn't you tell me, Emily...?" His voice trailed off. "You misled me."

I dropped to my knees and grabbed his shoulders, forcing him to look at me. "Lucas Walker. Listen to me now. There is nothing happening with Dom. I want you. Only you." I stare into his eyes.

He shakes his head, pulling his eyes away from mine. "I know he's still texting you," he says. "It doesn't sit right with me."

"Excuse me?" I blink, taken aback by his words. "What are you talking about?"

"Chloe told me about the texting," he spits out.

My heart drops to my stomach, and I suddenly understand Chloe's cryptic message earlier. She must have filled him in on her twisted version of events, which explains why he's been acting like this.

"Wait, Lucas," I stammer, desperate to explain. "I can—"

"Save it," he interrupts coldly, getting to his feet and walking away from me. "You think I don't know what's going on? You think I'm that stupid?"

"Lucas, you're not stupid," I say firmly, standing up and following him. "But you've got this all wrong. Let me explain."

"Fine," he snaps, rounding on me. "Explain. Tell me how you were going to tell me about Carlo. Or how you've been texting Dom behind my back."

"First of all," I start, feeling my own anger rising to match his. "I was planning on telling you about Carlo today, in person. I didn't want to dump that on you last night over the phone. I admit now that was a bad decision. I should have told you right away."

"How good of you." His voice drips with sarcasm.

"Lucas, don't," I warn, clenching my fists at my sides. "As for Dom, he texted me once. Last night. I don't know how he got my new number."

"Is that so?"

"Yes, it is!" I cry, frustration getting the better of me. "And you know what? I bet Chloe knew that too. She just chose to leave out certain details because she loves creating drama."

"Chloe?" He looks momentarily confused before his eyes narrow again. "You're trying to blame this on her now?"

"Think about it, Lucas," I implore him. "Why else would she have told you about Carlo and Dom? She's trying to drive a wedge between us."

He hesitates, clearly mulling over my words. The anger in his expression wavers, and for a moment, I see the vulnerable man beneath the tough exterior.

I reach for my phone and open the text from Dom.

"Here," I say, thrusting my phone into his hands, showing him the text message I sent before blocking him. "Read it for yourself." His eyes scan the screen, widening at the sight of the short and firm message: *Leave me alone.* "See?" I huff, snatching the phone back from him. "I wasn't hiding anything from you. I was just trying to deal with Dom myself."

He drops his gaze to the floor, his voice barely a whisper. "Fuck."

#

"Emily, I'm sorry," Lucas admits, his voice barely more than a whisper. "I should have trusted you. It's just that when Chloe mentioned Carlo and Dom, all in the same breath, I couldn't help but feel like something was off."

"Off?" I echo, raising an eyebrow. "You mean like Chloe deliberately stirring up drama between us?"

He drops his head back, with a groan.

"Look at the timing. She's made it clear she doesn't want us together and now this," I point out, crossing my arms over my chest. "I would have told you everything if I had a chance, but I couldn't reach you because you were so busy ghosting me."

"Ghosting you?" He winces, rubbing the back of his neck sheepishly. "Yeah, I guess I kind of was."

"Kind of?" I shoot back, but there's no real bite in my words. Instead, I can feel my anger starting to subside, replaced by a growing sense of relief that we're finally talking this through.

"Okay, fine," he admits with a rueful smile. "I was definitely ghosting you. I didn't know how else to handle it."

I reach out to touch his arm. "We need to trust each other and talk about these things. We can't let anyone come between us like that again."

"You're right," he says with a nod. "I'll handle Chloe's interference to make sure she doesn't try anything like that again." He smiles, wrapping his arms around me.

"Okay," I murmur into his chest. "I'll have to talk with her as well. The Dom attack was a low blow."

He squeezes me tighter. "Yeah, that one hit me hard, I won't lie. It made me question everything, even though I knew deep down that you wouldn't betray me like that. My composure just went out the window."

"That sucks that you had to go through that."

He pulls back slightly and looks into my face. "It's funny. The Carlo story made my head pop off, but as soon as she mentioned the Dom thing, that was a whole new level of obliteration."

He reaches for my face, drawing me closer to him in an irresistible magnetic pull. My heart flutters and I see his fingers twitch as if longing to touch my skin. His lips lightly brush my hair, as he inhales sharply, soaking in my scent. He wants me to let my guard down, I can see it in his eyes.

"Truce?" he asks, hovering closely.

My gaze flits between his, torn between a surging desire and a wave of uncertainty. But as he continues to hold me close, I feel my resistance melting away, replaced by an intensity that seems to mirror his own.

"Truce," I agree.

And he closes the distance between us, his lips meeting mine in a passionate kiss that seems to connect our souls. As his mouth moves on mine, our previous argument fades into oblivion, smothered by the intensity of our emotions. The pain and hurt from our pasts seem forgotten in our desire to be together. Our hands start exploring each other's bodies, craving the closeness that had felt so threatened.

The rhythm of the workout music envelops us, providing an illusion of privacy that lets us lose ourselves in each other's arms. The sensation of his lips on mine, the taste of him, is intoxicating. My fingers shake as I fumble with his shirt, my gaze locked with his.

"Lucas," I whisper, barely audible over the hum of the music, and I move my hands across his chest as he pulls his shirt over his head with one swift motion.

"God, Emily, I want you so bad," he breathes, his hands trembling as he yanks at the buttons of my blouse, revealing the delicate lace beneath.

As we continue to undress each other, each touch is like a spark igniting between us, building into a fire that feels like it could consume us both. He pushes me against the wall, pressing his body against mine, as I kick my jeans off and my bra falls to the floor.

"Touch me, Lucas," I plead, my body already aching with need. My breath is ragged as he runs his hands over my breasts, teasing each nipple with his thumbs. I gasp at the sudden pleasure that shoots through me. He lowers his hands, grasping the edges of my panties, and slips them down to my ankles, leaving me fully naked, and all I can think about is his touch.

He looks at me, catching his breath. "You're so fucking beautiful," he says, kissing me again. His hands continue their exploration, moving along my thighs and he presses my legs open with a push of his knee. I shudder as he reaches down and touches my wetness, sliding his fingers inside me while kissing my neck, causing me to moan. It feels incredible as he strokes me with maddening precision until I'm quivering.

In a swift motion, he lowers me onto my back on the mat, and I wrap my legs around him. He pulls off his boxers and I reach down and wrap my fingers around him, rubbing on his hardness and playing with the sensitive tip until he lets out a sharp moan of pleasure.

"Jesus, Emily," he gasps as he positions himself over me. I release him from my grasp, and he responds by pushing himself into me in one sensuous thrust.

My entire body tenses as I feel him fill me completely, pushing deeper, faster, and harder. He holds my knees, pressing them wider apart as he pounds into me. My breath pants through my lips as I arch my back, begging for more. He licks his fingers and reaches down for my most sensitive spot, tickling and flicking it as he continues to thrust inside me, and I lose my mind.

I cry out his name as waves of ecstasy crash over me, trembling beneath him as he moves inside me more powerfully than ever before. He continues to hold my knees apart and surges forward again and again, pushing into me until he cries out, his release reverberating throughout our bodies.

Gasping for air, he holds himself up over me, looking into my eyes in disbelief. I continue to hold him with my legs, refusing to let go, and he kisses my smiling lips with a gentle laugh.

"Holy shit," he whispers. "I think I saw God."

# Chapter Sixteen
## (Lucas)

Sitting in my office, the buzz of energy from the gym floor seeps through the walls—grunts of effort, thuds of bodies hitting mats, and the occasional shout, I think about last night with Emily on the mat in my apartment. It turned out to be the best session I'd ever had in my private ring. A guilty smile spreads across my lips as she sits across from me, her eyes locking on mine. I'm sure she knows what I'm thinking about, but her brows furrow from the current conversation: Carlo's threats to her and to Walker Enterprises.

"He had balls for approaching me like that," she says. "But he definitely had no idea he'd picked a target out of his league."

"Ha," I grunt. "You know it. He'll be more cautious in the future after going home with his tail between his legs." I huff. "He crossed a line, though, approaching you. And I consider it an act of aggression." My hands ball into fists under my desk.

For him to have approached my girl like that, when I wasn't around, was beyond disrespectful and calculated. My blood boiled just thinking about how he had the balls to go after her, making her feel unsafe and unprotected. It was just another part of his grand scheme to come at me.

"Don't worry about me, Lucas. I can handle that jerk." Her lightened tone doesn't make me forget the war this started, though. "I'm more concerned about your business. He's talking about poaching your top fighters. Offering them a stake in his gym and a hefty signing bonus."

I snort. As if a few extra bucks would convince my people to jump ship. They're loyal. "Let him try. He won't get far."

She shifts nervously, still not convinced that I'm not threatened by this asshole.

"He's also saying awful things about you and Walker Enterprises. Trying to damage your reputation." Her eyes flash with anger. "We need to stop him before he sinks his claws in too deep."

"I'll handle Carlo," I say. "If anything, I need to turn it back on him."

"His fighters' reputations for bad sportsmanship and illegal drug use could be a weakness we can target," she says, tapping her pen against the desk. "We just need to make sure your own fighters are squeaky clean and represent the best you have to offer."

"Agreed." I rub my chin thoughtfully. "But Carlo's a snake, and he won't stop at anything to get what he wants. We just need to be prepared for anything now."

"Like assaulting women in dark parking lots?" she mutters, her face hardening at the memory.

"Exactly," I say, gritting my teeth. "I'll double down on security for the gym. And honestly, I need to keep a closer eye on you. You've got yourself a stalker."

"True. But more importantly, we can't let him win," she says firmly.

I smile, appreciating her dedication to the gym, to the company... to me.

"Speaking of winning," she continues, "I managed to secure some new sponsorships for the Dubai expo. They'll definitely help increase our visibility and attract more investors."

"Really?" I lean back in my chair, thoroughly impressed. "You never cease to amaze me, Em. I have to admit, the recent rapid growth of Walker Enterprises is largely thanks to you."

She shakes her head and keeps her eyes down as if it were nothing. But I know how much I owe to her.

"Speaking of growth," she says, glancing down at her phone as it buzzes with a new notification. "I just got a new bid from someone who wants me to negotiate their contracts. Things are getting back on track for my business too."

A darkness settles over me almost instantly. "Another client trying to poach you away?" I ask, unable to keep the hint of jealousy from my tone. Emily's negotiating skills are in high demand, and more than one competitor has attempted to lure her from Walker Enterprises with an irresistible offer, so I'm not crazy to worry a little.

"It's nothing." She waves her hand dismissively. "Just someone wanting to discuss a new campaign."

I feel my blood pressure rising and am not fully sure why. It just feels like I don't want to share her anymore, but I know that's not up to me. I still can't help it, though.

"If they're offering you something I'm not, I want to know about it." I shoot her a stern look, watching as she fidgets beneath my gaze. "I think it's time you took on more here, instead. You deserve a stake in this company, Em. Hell, you're responsible for a huge portion of our growth over the past year. Name your price."

"Lucas, I—"

"Name it." I brace my hands on the desk, leaning towards her. "I want your full service, and I'm willing to pay for it. No more running off with other clients or wondering where your loyalties lie."

"I'm not disloyal." Her eyes flash, color rising in her cheeks. "I have a life and career outside of Walker Enterprises, or have you forgotten?"

"This isn't just business anymore." The words slip out before I can stop them. I straighten, clearing my throat.

"Lucas...," she begins, her eyes darting between me and her phone screen. "It's just a proposal. I haven't agreed to anything yet."

"Yet." The word hangs in the air like a challenge, my temper rising as insecurities claw at me. "So, you're considering it? You're thinking about taking on another client?"

"Maybe I'm weighing my options," she retorts, her eyebrows arching defiantly.

"Options?" I scoff, the muscle in my jaw twitching. "What happened to being committed to this partnership? To us?"

"Us? That's not what this is about. Business is business, Lucas," she insists, trying to sound in control, but I can see the uncertainty in her eyes. "It doesn't mean I'm not committed to you or Walker Enterprises."

"Doesn't it?" My voice raises an octave, the heat of anger simmering beneath the surface. "If you're still entertaining other offers, that tells me you're not fully committed."

"Don't be ridiculous," she snaps.

"Then why even consider it?" The words burst out of me like an explosion, my hands smacking down on the desk. "It doesn't fit with our relationship."

"Relationship?" she repeats incredulously, her voice laced with disbelief. "This is about work, not our relationship."

"Work is part of our relationship," I argue, my chest heaving. "And right now, it feels like you're not all in."

"Maybe…." She hesitates, her voice wavering ever so slightly. "Maybe I'm just trying to figure out where I fit in all this, Lucas."

She stares at me with a vulnerable gaze, but I'm too wound up to back down.

"Well, figure it out," I growl, the words dripping with frustration. "Just don't expect me to sit here and watch you walk away from everything now."

"No one's walking away," she snaps, her eyes flashing with defiance. "This doesn't mean I'm not committed to you or our relationship."

"Then why won't you just refuse the offer?" I demand, my chest tightening. "If you're really committed, then show it by turning them down."

"Lucas, that's not how this works," she replies exasperatedly, throwing her hands up in the air. "I've given so much to help build this business, but that doesn't mean I have to give up every other opportunity that comes my way."

"Every other opportunity?" I snarl, stepping closer to her. "Like Dom? Is he part of these 'opportunities' too?"

The second his name leaves my mouth, I regret saying it. But I can't help but feel threatened by that asshole. He keeps popping up in her life and I know how amazing she is. Of course, he would want her back.

The mention of Dom seems to be the last straw for Emily. She jumps to her feet and leans over my desk, her face contorted with anger, and she glares at me, eyes blazing.

"Don't you ever speak to me like that again!" Her teeth grind together through each word. "Dom has nothing to do with any of this and you know it!" she yells, her voice cracking. "This is about me and my career, not some stupid rivalry between you two!"

"Stupid rivalry?" I practically shout, my anger reaching a boiling point. "You think that's all this is? Just a stupid rivalry between two men fighting over you?"

"Maybe if you spent less time worrying about him and more time focusing on us, we wouldn't be having this conversation!" she retorts.

"Fine!" I snap, my patience finally wearing thin. "If that's what you want, then go! Go chase after your precious clients!"

"Fine!" she screams back, flying out of my office and slamming the door behind her.

#

It didn't take long before I knew I'd fucked up, five seconds maybe. It was my fucking insecurity rising up again. I didn't want to lose her, and everywhere I looked there was another threat. But this time, I wasn't going to allow my life to fall to pieces.

My feet move on their own as I follow her out of my office and into the gym.

"Emily, wait!" I call out, catching up with her as she storms through the gym, heading toward the lady's locker room, ignoring my plea.

"Leave me alone, Lucas!" she shouts back, her voice raw with emotion. The fighters in the gym pause their training, their attention drawn to the spectacle.

"Look, I'm sorry," I say, my anger subsiding slightly as I approach her. "Let's just talk about this, okay?"

"Talk?" She whirls around, her eyes flashing with fury. "You had your chance to talk in there. Instead, you decided to throw Dom in my face!"

"Because I'm worried about you, Emily!" I shout, my frustration rising once more. "I don't want you getting involved with him or anyone else who might take you away from me!"

She scoffs, her hands flying up in exasperation. "Is that what this is really about? Your possessiveness?"

"Maybe it is!" I admit, my heart beating out of control. "I don't want to lose you, Emily."

"Then trust me," she begs, her voice breaking. "Trust me to make my own decisions and to not abandon you."

"Can you honestly tell me you haven't thought about it?" I ask, my voice laced with doubt.

Her eyes narrow, and she crosses her arms over her chest defensively. "No, I've thought about it. That's what people do in business—they weigh their options. But I've always chosen you, Lucas. And I always will."

"Prove it," I say, my voice a low growl as I pin her against the wall, my face inches from hers, huffing into her face.

She turns away, refusing to meet my gaze. "Get off me," she demands, her tone icy.

"Say it, Emily," I insist, keeping her shoulders pinned to the wall. "Tell me you're committed to this."

In one swift motion, she pushes against my shoulder, and her leg sweeps behind my knee, causing me to lose my balance and stumble. The fighters around us erupt into cheers and applause, calling out her name, as she uses the most basic jujitsu move against me.

"Get back, Walker!" she blasts, panting. "Is that proof enough for you?" she asks, her eyes blazing with determination.

I stare at her, a mix of admiration and annoyance swirling within me. She's stubborn and infuriating, but she's also passionate and loyal. And in that moment, I realize just how much I need her in my life—not just as a business partner, but as my woman who makes me a better man.

"She's got you beat, Coach," one of the fighters calls out, followed by laughter.

I can't help but grin like a fool, accepting defeat. She's proven her point, and honestly, I've never been more attracted to her.

"Alright, you win," I say, my voice light. Ignoring the mocking insults coming from my fighters, I stride over to her and scoop her up off her feet, tossing her onto my shoulder.

"Put me down!" she squeals, half-annoyed, half-amused as I carry her back to my office, our audience still hooting and clapping behind us.

Once inside, I set her down gently on the couch and lean against my desk, catching my breath. She crosses her arms, feigning annoyance, but I can see the corners of her mouth twitching.

"Emily, you're a difficult woman and a pain in my ass," I admit, running a hand over my hair. "But I think I finally figured out what the hell is wrong with me."

Her eyebrows shoot up. "Oh? And what's that?"

Allowing the honesty of my words to release all of my pent-up tension and fear, I blurt out, "I'm in love with you."

# Chapter Seventeen
## (Emily)

Sitting on the couch in Lucas's office, my jaw hits the floor from his unexpected words. It's like I'm frozen for a moment, shocked by his honesty and raw admission.

Taking a deep breath, I look into his eyes and say, "I love you too, Lucas." The words feel good coming out of my mouth. They'd been held in for so long. "I've been waiting for you to figure it out. I didn't want to pressure you with my own feelings."

Relief washes over his face, and a lopsided grin spreads across his lips. "Damn, I wish you had," he chuckles. "I would've figured things out a lot faster." We both laugh, and the tension between us evaporates. In that moment, everything feels right.

Lucas steps closer and reaches for my hands, lifting me to my feet. His strong grip holds me by my waist as he leans in for a tender kiss. Our lips meet, and it feels like coming home. The taste of him is familiar and comforting, yet still sends shivers down my spine. We pull apart slowly, our eyes locking on to each other's.

"Emily," he murmurs against my lips. My heart swells at the sound of my name, and I know that this is where I belong—with Lucas, finally admitting our feelings to one another.

As we stand there, wrapped up in each other's arms, it feels like everything has finally fallen into place.

The echo of whistles and thuds from the gym infiltrates our peaceful bubble, forcing us to face reality once again. Reluctantly, we pull away from each other, a small sigh escaping my lips.

"Guess duty calls," Lucas says, quickly refocusing on the work being done in the gym.

"Go, fearless leader," I say with a teasing grin. "I'll just grab my stuff out of the locker room. I have some errands to run."

"Deal," he replies, planting one last quick kiss on my forehead before striding off toward the mats.

#

I make my way to the women's locker room, trying to shake off the swirling mixture of emotions coursing through me. As I enter the quiet space, I'm hit with the familiar scent of lavender air freshener and the sight of gray metal lockers. I head to my usual spot, the one right by the sinks, and open the squeaky door to retrieve my bag.

As I rummage through the contents of my locker, I replay the conversation with Lucas in my head. It feels surreal—like a dream I never knew I had. My heart swells, and I find myself wanting to laugh out loud at the absurdity of it all. After months of tiptoeing around each other, we finally had the courage to admit our feelings and it feels amazing.

My fingers wrap around the strap of my bag as I close the locker door, excitement in my veins.

I take a deep breath, trying to steady my racing heart as I lean against the row of sinks and stare at my reflection in the mirror. With flushed cheeks and eyes shining, it's evident just how much Lucas's confession has affected me.

"Emily," his deep, husky voice comes up behind me, making me jump.

"Lucas!" I exclaim, my hand flying to my chest as I spin around to face him. "You scared me!"

"Sorry for sneaking up on you," he says, stepping closer with a teasing grin. "I just couldn't resist following you in here, knowing there are no other women on site."

I exhale, lowering my shoulders, and I turn back to the sink to grab my things, keeping my eyes on him in the reflection.

"Are you always this stealthy?" I ask, my voice wavering.

"Only when it involves you, apparently," he chuckles, closing the distance between us, wrapping his arms around my waist. His eyes meet mine in the mirror, and the intensity in his gaze sends shivers through me.

"You look absolutely beautiful right now," he murmurs, his breath warm on my neck as he leans in and trails his lips along it. The sensation of his mouth on my skin makes me weak in the knees, and I tilt my head, hoping for more.

"That's nice," I whisper, clutching the edge of the sink for support as my legs threaten to give out beneath me. "Please don't stop." I need him close, need to feel his body like I've never needed anything before.

He smiles against my neck, planting another gentle kiss there before moving up to trail featherlight kisses along my jawline. My breath catches in my throat, and my grip on the sink tightens.

I turn to face him, and he pulls me against his chest as we kiss more passionately.

"God, I've wanted this with you for so long," he murmurs between kisses, his hands running down my back and gripping my hips.

"Me too," I whisper, as the world outside the locker room fades away, leaving only the two of us together.

My heart races as I respond to Lucas's advances, our mouths and hands exploring each other. His fingers find the hem of my top, tugging it up and over my head before tossing it aside.

My bra quickly follows, and then his calloused hands move over my bare breasts, pinching and teasing my nipples until I'm writhing against him. "You make me crazy," he murmurs, tugging my nipples and sending a jolt of pleasure straight to my core.

I reach for the button of his jeans, fumbling to gain access to him. He chuckles, catching my hands before undoing his pants and pushing them down his hips along with his boxers. He removes my jeans in a blink and painstakingly slides my panties down my legs.

The sight of him, hard and ready for me, makes me quiver. I lick my lips, aching for him to take me on the sink, but instead, he scoops me into his arms.

Carrying me into the nearest shower stall, he turns on the spray, warm water cascading over our heated skin. I moan at the sensation, moving my hands over his wet hair and bringing his mouth back to mine.

He braces one hand on the wall above my head, the other sliding between my legs to stroke my wetness. I gasp against his lips, rocking my hips to press into his touch. "You're so fucking hot," he growls, sliding two fingers into me as my back arches. "You're ready for me, baby," he moans.

"Yes," I cry, beyond words now. I need him, need to feel him moving inside me. "Lucas, please."

He withdraws his fingers and hitches my leg around his hip, positioning himself at my entrance. Our eyes meet, dark desire and love swirling in his gaze, and he eases inside me with a groan.

I arch into him, clinging tightly as he begins to move. The rhythm is slow but deep, each stroke sending sparks of pleasure through my entire body.

"Emily," he breathes, burying his face in my neck. "I love you so much."

And we lose ourselves in each other, our bodies and souls entwining like never before. The love we've kept hidden for so long finally takes flight, and it's everything I ever wanted.

Our gasps echo in the stall as he moves faster in me. Holding my leg at his hip, he opens me further, looking down at my exposed pink flesh as he pushes into me, water running over us. His breath grows deeper and faster as his arousal hits oblivion, sending me into spasms that make me cry out.

He can't hold on any longer and pushes into me, hard, as his body tenses, grasping onto me with all his might. He shudders as the last of him blasts into me, causing us both to crumple beneath the warm water spray.

As our heartbeats begin to slow and our breathing returns to normal, he kisses me gently, pushing my wet hair away from my face.

"You're everything I want," he whispers.

I take in the moment, knowing it feels like a fairy tale, or like we're in a movie. My heart is so content with him and as a lover, holy shit, he's perfection. I've never been so comfortable with sex before, but with him, I just let it all out. It's an amazing feeling.

Eventually, knowing we must return to reality, Lucas carefully sets me back on my feet and turns off the water. He steps out of the shower stall first, sneaking a glance around the locker room to make sure the coast is clear before motioning for me to follow.

"Come on," he whispers with a guilty grin, holding out his hand. I nod, taking his hand and stepping out of the shower.

He quickly wraps a towel around me, using the corner to pat my face dry.

We tiptoe through the locker room, hearts pounding with adrenaline as we find our clothes strewn across the tile floor. Dressing quickly, we giggle, trying to appear as nonchalant as possible, even though I know we're far from it.

"See you out there," he says, planting a firm kiss on my mouth, his eyes twinkling with mischief.

I watch as he squares his shoulders with an air of confidence as he slips out the locker room door. Waiting a few moments to be safe, I finally make my way back to his office, trying to appear inconspicuous. With every step, my heart races as I replay the steamy shower scene in my head, nearly tripping myself.

As I walk in, Lucas looks up and gives me a knowing smile. "Hey," he says softly.

"Hey," I reply, willing myself not to blush.

And as we enjoy our guilty exchange, Xavier saunters in, a smirk on his face that makes it clear he knows something's up. I can't help but squirm under his gaze, feeling like a teenager caught making out in her parents' basement.

"Have you two been enjoying yourselves?" Xavier teases, chuckling at our obvious discomfort.

"Shut up," Lucas mutters, his cheeks tinged red.

He grins. "Hey, man, I just wanted you to know that Daniel had to leave for an appointment, but he'll be back later. We're working on a killer move that's sure to wow."

Lucas smiles. "Ya, man, sounds good."

Before I can think of something witty to add, Chloe bursts into the room like a tornado, clutching a tray of coffees in her hands.

"Peace offering!" she announces in a sing-song voice, setting the tray down with a smack. "I come bearing caffeine and apologies."

I catch my breath from her unexpected appearance, knowing the last time I saw her was when my entire world fell apart. She'd "misinformed" Lucas about my interactions with Carlo and Dom, leading him down a path of unnecessary pain and insecurity.

"Apologies for what?" I ask cautiously, trying to gauge her mood.

"Ugh, for being a drama queen," she admits, rolling her eyes at herself. "I shouldn't have interfered with your relationship or tried to control you guys. I'm a bitch for that."

My eyes widen in shock. "Chloe, it's okay," I reassure her, exchanging a glance with Lucas.

"Still," she insists, handing me a coffee. "I just want everyone to be happy."

"Thanks, Chloe," Lucas says sincerely, accepting his coffee. "We appreciate it."

"Great," she beams, clapping her hands together. "Now that we've got that settled, can we please focus on the important stuff? Like making sure my wedding doesn't turn into a complete disaster?"

I let out a small chuckle. "Of course," I agree, smirking at Lucas who is trying to hide his amusement.

"We certainly wouldn't want that, now would we," he says, a mischievous glint in his eye.

Chloe swats his arm in feigned offense.

"Seriously, though, guys, you two look great together," she gushes. "I can tell you're good for each other. I mean, Lucas, I haven't seen you this relaxed in ages."

He wiggles his eyebrows at me, reminding me of our locker room encounter.

"Very true," he says, his eyes never leaving mine. "I'm glad you suggested we work together."

She grins, lifting one shoulder to her ear. "Aw, you guys are giving me all the feels!" she exclaims, wiping away fake tears.

"Okay, enough mushy stuff," I tease, feeling my cheeks flush. "Let's get back to wedding planning."

"Fine," Chloe relents, rolling her eyes playfully. "But just know that I'm making an effort to come around. I support both of you."

"Thanks, Chloe," Lucas replies.

As Chloe and I instantly get lost in wedding planning conversation, I can't help but sneak glances at Lucas every now and then. Seeing the happiness on his face and the way he looks at me makes my heart soar. And as Chloe watches, I can tell she's keeping an open mind to what is happening between us.

"Alright," she announces, clapping her hands together again. "Now that we're all back on the same page, maybe I can sleep again." She grabs her purse and throws her empty coffee cup in the trash. "Emily, girl's night out this week. I won't take no for an answer," she demands as she barrels out the door, leaving papers flying in her wake.

# Chapter Eighteen
## (Lucas)

The gym pulses with raw energy as Xavier spars with his closest match, Daniel, their bodies moving fluidly across the mat. Sweat drips from furrowed brows as they grapple and twist, each seeking an advantage over the other. I feel the tension in the air, electric and charged, as Emily stands beside me, her eyes locked on the fighters and her fingers tapping against her thigh.

With the gentle sway of the gym lights overhead, we watch from the edge of the mat as Xavier shifts position with Daniel, his strength evident in his bulging biceps, making him a formidable opponent.

With a quick move, Xavier sweeps Daniel's defenses aside and slides an arm under his neck, while his other arm wraps around to secure the hold, cutting off the blood flow to the brain. When Xavier executes the move, it's a thing of lethal beauty, a seamless flow of power and precision.

My heart leaps—that's the move that's going to win us notoriety in Dubai.

Emily gasps beside me and her fingers tighten around my arm.

Xavier finally releases Daniel from the hold and the two of them stand, straightening their rash guards and wiping sweat from their brows.

"Excellent," I call to them. "That's the winning ticket."

They smile, knowing the practice of the Rear Naked Choke, and a few of the other moves I've taught will define them as top fighters in Dubai. During a quick break, I lean down and murmur in Emily's ear, "I think we might really have a chance."

She looks up at me with a knowing grin. "Yeah, me too. In more ways than one."

I look at her, eyebrows pulled in.

"You know," she continues. "We have a chance with Chloe now too." She shakes her head in disbelief. "I mean, her sudden change of heart about us is, like, wow."

I chuckle, remembering how Chloe had cornered us in my office, gushing about us being together now. "I suppose it's a good thing she's on board, though," I admit. "Takes some pressure off knowing we have her support."

"Definitely," she agrees with a grin. "She was getting a little difficult to manage for a minute there."

"For a minute?" I laugh.

Then my attention shifts back to Xavier and Daniel as they move back to the mat preparing to launch back into their spar. I watch their movements, analyzing every twist and turn. "You see that?" I ask Emily, pointing at Xavier's technique. "That right there makes him a monster. He's going to earn major recognition in Dubai."

"Amazing," she breathes, eyes riveted on him. "You've trained these guys so well. And more than just fighting. It's like a brotherhood."

I stare at her, shocked at how much she's read into the practice. "Exactly." And it settles deep within me that we are all in exactly the right place. "It's true. We all depend on each other in every way. That move there—"

"Lucas!" The shout cuts through the gym, obnoxious and grating. Carlo saunters in, flanked by two of his cronies, smirking like the cat who swallowed the canary. His presence instantly sours the atmosphere, transforming the once vibrant space into something dark and suffocating.

"Carlo," I growl, my fingers curling into fists at my side. "What the hell do you want?"

"Rumor has it you've been cheating, Lucas," he taunts, his voice dripping with malice. "Falsifying records, misrepresenting your fighters' skills. You're not playing fair, and I think everyone should know."

"Get out of here, Carlo. You're full of shit," I snap, anger boiling beneath my skin. "You're making it up as you go."

He moves closer toward the mat. "Did you honestly think you'd get away with it?" he continues, ignoring my warning. "You may have fooled a few people for a while, but the truth always comes out. And when it does"—he smirks—"your little jujitsu empire is going to crumble."

Emily bristles beside me, her earlier lightheartedness gone. "Get him out of here. He's only trying to make trouble and he's not worth it."

She's right. I just need to keep my temper under control and get rid of this vermin so we can get back to training. But as expected, my heart is pounding in my throat as my vision turns to laser focus on him.

"Carlo, for the last time"—my voice shakes with barely restrained rage—"get the fuck out of my gym." I feel Emily's hand on my arm, trying to ground me.

He smirks, turning his gaze toward her. "What's the matter, Lucas? Can't handle a little competition?" His eyes travel up and down her body, lingering inappropriately. "Or maybe you're just distracted by your latest plaything here. She is rather tempting."

That's it. I can't take it anymore. As soon as he shifted his foul mouth to her, my mission became very clear.

My fists clench as white-hot fury courses through me, and I lunge at him. Our bodies collide, and we grapple with each other, both of us highly trained black belts refusing to tap out. And right now, there's no refined technique or strategic finesse, it's all raw anger and adrenaline.

As we roll and twist on the mat, I manage to get the upper hand, trapping Carlo in a chokehold. But he quickly counters, slipping free and forcing me into a defensive position. Our limbs become a tangled mess as we continue to trade blows, each of us fighting for dominance.

The other fighters in the gym gather around us, their expressions filled with shock as they watch their mentors battle it out. They hover at the edge of the mat, unsure whether to intervene or let us continue.

Some call out encouragement, while others just stare, unsure of what to make of the situation.

In the midst of the chaos, my thoughts race. What the hell am I doing? This isn't me. I'm not some hot-headed brawler who loses control at such ridiculous provocation. I need to regain control, but it feels nearly impossible with every fiber of my being screaming for blood.

My focus narrows to just me and Carlo, each strike, grapple, and countermove a war between rivals. Sweat pours from my brow, and my muscles scream with exertion, but the pain only fuels my determination to win. My inner thoughts are a swirling mix of anger and fear, but I don't dare let them surface.

And then, as I narrowly dodge another of Carlo's strikes, something inside me snaps. Suddenly, I'm not in the gym anymore—I'm back in the heat of combat, surrounded by the sounds of gunfire and chaos. My heart races, threatening to burst from my chest, and I struggle to breathe.

"Lucas, stop!" Emily shouts again, her voice desperate. But I can't hear her over the pounding of my heart and the thunder of adrenaline coursing through my veins. Her eyes are wide with concern, and it's enough to remind me of what's at stake.

Carlo takes advantage of my momentary lapse in concentration, landing a solid blow to my ribs. I wince but manage to counter with a well-placed knee strike, sending him sprawling. As he struggles to regain his footing, I force myself to step back, breathing heavily.

I barely register Xavier's strong grip on my arm as he pulls me away from the mat.

I glance over at Carlo, panting and battered, and the reality of what I'd allowed to happen begins to sink in, and I feel a wave of shame wash over me.

"Enough," I pant, my body aching from the intense exchange. "Get the fuck out of my gym, Carlo. And if you ever"—I jab a finger in his direction—"come near Emily or try to sabotage my business again, I promise you won't walk away so easily."

He glares at me, rage still burning in his eyes, but finally relents, limping toward the door as his posse follows suit. He turns one last time and shouts, "I told you he was crazy!"

As the gym doors slam shut behind them, I let out a long exhale, feeling the weight of my actions pressing down on me.

"Lucas," Emily says softly, checking on my condition, knowing it has nothing to do with my physical well-being. "Are you okay?"

"No," I admit, shaking. "I'm not."

#

Sitting on the bench outside the gym, Emily encourages me to take deep breaths of fresh air, but the familiar symptoms hit me like a tidal wave. My heart pounds wildly, sweat dripping down my back. The sounds of the fight echo in my head, Carlo's taunts mingling with the ghostly screams of comrades lost long ago.

I grip Emily's shoulder, the solid warmth of her body is the only thing anchoring me to the present. She wraps an arm around my waist, murmuring soothing words I can't quite make out over the rushing in my ears.

Xavier comes out a few minutes later, worry etched into the frown on his usually cheerful face. "Boss, you alright?"

I give a jerky nod, not trusting my voice. He sees right through it, though, having been with me through some of my worst episodes. He's a steady presence offering silent support.

"Do you need me to call your doctor?" Emily asks softly. "They might have a solution to help you relax."

I shake my head, spine rigid as I fight the urge to hide until the panic passes.

And in the same breath, Carlo and his fighters emerge from the side of the parking lot, all sneers and jeers. "Looks like you need a stretcher, old man!" Carlo calls. "PTSD acting up again? Maybe it's time to pack it in!"

Red haze clouds my vision from the taunts, rage boiling up to replace the fear. I surge forward but Emily and Xavier catch me before I can pummel Carlo's smug face.

"Lucas, no!" Emily yells, grabbing my arm and yanking me back with surprising force. I stumble, the sudden motion jolting me out of the flashback's grip.

Chest heaving, I stare at my clenched fist as the anger drains away, leaving me shaken. Carlo's laughter fades into the distance as he walks away, but the damage is already done. I've given him exactly what he wanted, proof of my instability for the world to see.

"Asshole," Xavier murmurs, walking with Emily and me toward my SUV.

Emily opens the passenger door, concern etched on her brow. "I'm taking you home," she says firmly, leaving no room for argument. Not that I have the energy to protest.

The familiar rumble of the engine soothes my frayed nerves during the drive to my apartment. We ride in silence as I continue my attempt to gain control. When we enter my building, Emily stays by my side, keeping a steadying hand on my arm as we ride the elevator to the penthouse.

"Do you need anything?" she asks once we're inside. "Water? Food?"

I shake my head, making a beeline for the treadmill. The only thing that will calm the restless energy thrumming through my veins is pushing my body to the brink.

Emily hesitates by the couches, worry shadowing her face. "Lucas, are you sure you should be exercising right now? Your heart's already racing."

"I'm fine," I grit out, punching the start button with more force than necessary. The treadmill hums to life and I break into a run, ignoring the burn in my legs as I push the speed higher and higher.

Emily hovers at the edge of my vision, arms crossed over her chest, frown deepening with every increase of the speed gauge. I know I should stop to reassure her, but I can't seem to slow my pace. All I can see is Carlo's smug grin and hear his mocking laughter, fueling my determination to outrun the memories.

The speedometer ticks past twelve miles per hour, my heart thundering to match the pace. Emily throws her hands up, clearly realizing she won't be able to talk sense into me.

"At least take it easy, will you?" she snaps, dropping onto the sofa. Her presence is oddly soothing despite her obvious annoyance.

I steal a quick glance at her, the brief distraction causing my stride to falter. She's watching me like a hawk, gaze worried and wary. I wonder if she's rethinking her decision to stick by my side through episodes like this and if she's finally grasping what she's signed up for by choosing to love a man as damaged as me. The thought makes my chest ache with a pain that has nothing to do with my protesting lungs. I pour on more speed, hoping to outrun that particular demon too.

My legs burn as I push past thirteen miles per hour, sweat dripping down my spine. I feel Emily's gaze boring into me, silently urging me to stop before I do permanent damage, but I ignore it. If I stop now, the memories and self-doubts will overtake me. I have to keep moving.

"Lucas, come on. That's enough." Emily's voice is sharp with worry. I risk another glance at her, seeing the frown etched into her pretty features, and my resolve wavers. I can't stand being the cause of that look, not when she deserves so much better.

With a muttered curse, I slap the emergency stop button, legs buckling as the treadmill belt slows to a stop. I clutch the handrails to remain upright, chest heaving as I gulp in air. My pulse continues to race even as my body stills, flashes of violence playing on a loop behind my eyelids.

But then, gentle hands grasp my face, tilting it. I blink open my eyes to find Emily peering up at me, her expression soft with compassion.

"You're okay," she murmurs. "Just breathe. I'm right here."

Her words pierce through the haze of panic and memory, grounding me in the present. I draw a shaky breath, then another, matching the rhythm of her thumbs stroking my cheekbones. Slowly but surely, my heart rate begins to settle into a more normal pace.

## Chapter Nineteen
### (Emily)

The bustle of downtown Boston thrums around us as Chloe prattles on about centerpieces and seating charts. The city is alive with the sounds of laughter and chatter as tourists and locals enjoy the fresh afternoon air.

"Okay, so we've got to finalize the seating chart and pick out the menu," Chloe announces. Her voice is full of excitement, but my thoughts keep drifting back to Lucas. "There will be hell to pay if I sit the Ohioans anywhere near my Southie cousins."

I let out a small chuckle, imagining the chaos that would ensue between her wacky relatives. "No doubt. We're going to need to find someplace that serves caffeine so we can sit and talk about it," I suggest, steering her towards a nearby coffeehouse. Inside, the rich aroma of freshly brewed coffee fills the air as we settle into a pair of worn leather armchairs.

Chloe opens her wedding planning notebook, revealing a detailed seating chart that would impress even the most seasoned event planner. "So, here's what I'm thinking," she begins, pointing to various names on the chart. "We'll put Aunt Connie next to Uncle Joe, because they haven't seen each other in years, and we all know how much they love to gossip."

"Sounds perfect," I agree, suppressing an eye roll. "What about the menu? Have you decided on that yet?"

"Almost," Chloe says, biting her lip. "I just can't decide between the sea bass or the beef tenderloin for the main course. What if someone has allergies or is gluten intolerant? I swear, if someone calls 9-1-1…. Can you imagine the disaster?"

"Chloe, relax," I laugh. "I'm sure whatever you choose will be delicious and no one will end up in the hospital."

She grins sheepishly, acknowledging the ridiculousness of her fears.

The idea of a hospital makes me think back to Lucas again. My worry continues to grow each day he stays in his apartment, away from the gym, away from outside interactions. He's not getting any better and I'm beginning to fear for his future.

"Okay, you're right. I'm overthinking it," she admits. "But, seriously, what if there's a huge fight at the reception over something silly like who gets the last piece of cake or who's the better drunken dancer? I'd die of embarrassment!"

The mention of a fight leaves me no choice but to tell Chloe. She needs to know what happened to Lucas and honestly, I can use her support right now. I just don't know what to do anymore.

"Speaking of fights," I say hesitantly. "There was an incident with Lucas recently, at the gym." I press my lips together. "With Carlo."

Chloe gasps, her eyes wide. "Fuck! I knew something was going to go wrong. What happened? Did Lucas hurt someone?"

Her response sent my mind spiraling, almost like she assumed Lucas did something bad, like he was the aggressor.

"Actually, it was Carlo's doing," I state plainly. "He instigated the entire thing, attacking Lucas with a bunch of lies," I explain. "Lucas lost his cool and they fought." Chloe's eyes grow wider. "It was a draw, but, seriously, Lucas could have killed him if he wanted to. It got pretty intense."

"Wow," she breathes, shaking her head in disbelief. "I never would have expected that from him. I thought he was controlling that stuff better." She glances down. "I'm glad he didn't seriously hurt Carlo, though. That would have been awful for both of them."

"Same," I agree. "But the problem is, he's not recovering from the fight."

She sits up straight. "He's hurt?"

"Not physically," I murmur. "It's his PTSD now. The worst I've ever seen. He won't leave the apartment."

She lowers her eyes to the creamy swirls in her coffee as the barista places the mugs on our table. "I've seen that happen to him before, when he first got back."

"Really? What happened?" I press for details. "How did he get better?" I ask, needing information so I can help him somehow. I exhale, feeling a weight lift off my chest as I finally share my fears with someone else and they know what I'm talking about.

She shrugs and presses her lips to the side. "Time, I think. I literally had no clue what to do. He just kind of figured it out for himself."

I swallow hard, realizing I wasn't getting any answers, and now knowing how alone he's been in all of this.

As if on cue, our server appears again at our table, oblivious to the seriousness of our conversation. "Would you ladies like any more cream or cocoa powder for your coffee? And are you ready to order something more substantial?"

"Uh, sure, I'll take some cream," I mumble distractedly, glancing at the menu without really seeing it. "And I guess we'll split a croissant."

"Excellent choice," the server replies cheerfully before disappearing back into the bustling café.

"Em, I have to be honest," Chloe says quietly once he's gone. "I have absolutely no idea how to help someone experiencing PTSD. I feel so useless."

I know she's already overwhelmed with her wedding, and the people-pleaser in me stands up, always being the one in our friendship to find the true solutions. "Don't worry, Chloe. I'll help him. I have an idea that might be really good for him."

She reaches for her coffee, her eyes brimming with gratitude. "I can't thank you enough for being there for him," she says, sincerity lacing every word. "And I'm sorry if I've taken you for granted lately with all my wedding craziness. You've been a real lifesaver."

"Hey, it's okay," I say, giving her a warm smile. "Your bridezilla moments have been pretty entertaining."

A chuckle escapes her lips before she takes a sip of her coffee, the corners of her eyes crinkling in amusement. "Oh, you don't even know the half of it," she admits with a shake of her head. "But seriously, Em, you're amazing. You're exactly what Lucas needs right now."

"Thanks. That means a lot." I take a deep breath, steeling myself for what I know I have to do next. It's time to put everything else aside and focus on helping Lucas—no matter what that entails.

"Okay, listen," I begin, assertiveness taking over my tone. "We're going to make a change of plans for today. Forget about the seating chart and the menu for now—we need to concentrate on finding a way to help Lucas."

Chloe's eyebrows shoot up in surprise, her initial resistance evident. "But, Em, the wedding is just around the corner, and we still have so much to do."

"Lucas is our priority now, Chlo," I insist, my determination unwavering. "He needs us more than ever, and we can't let him down."

She hesitates for a moment, clearly torn between her loyalty to her brother and the approaching wedding. But then, as realization dawns on her face, she nods in agreement. "You're right, Em. Lucas needs our help. So, what's your big idea?"

I sit back in my leather armchair planning my next moves with a satisfied smile.

\#

With our coffee cups empty and the croissant demolished, we leave the bustling café behind and head off on our mission to save Lucas. And as we walk side by side through the busy streets of Boston, I can't help but feel a surge of hope. My plan is a good one and I believe it has the power to work.

"First, let me make a quick call," I say, pulling out my phone and dialing the number for the dog shelter. I know how much Lucas bonded with Charlie during our last visit—maybe spending some time with him and his wagging tail will help ease his symptoms.

"Hey, Jayne. It's Emily," I greet the manager when she picks up. "I'm on my way over and was wondering about Charlie. Is there any way he might be able to make a home visit to Lucas today?"

"Hey, Em, of course. Charlie would love that," she replies without hesitation. "Just come on by, and we'll get him all set for the visit."

My heart fills with excitement. "Perfect. Thank you, Jayne. We'll be there soon." I hang up the phone, turning back to Chloe with a determined smile. "Wait 'til you meet this dog. Lucas loves him."

"Um, okay," Chloe stutters, having little experience with canines, and even less of shelters, but her smile reflects her renewed sense of purpose. "I trust you."

As we make our way through the maze of high-rises, my adrenaline climbs with the hope that Charlie will be exactly what Lucas needs. Once the sign for the shelter comes into view, I point it out to Chloe and she slows, baring her teeth.

"Do they bite?" she asks, hesitantly.

I let out a laugh. "Only if you do first."

And we head in with anticipation oozing from our grins. The moment we walk in, the air is filled with the excited barks and whines of hopeful animals. Chloe's hand covers her nose instinctively as the overwhelming smells assault her senses.

"Emily!" Jayne exclaims as she spots us, her face lighting up with a warm smile. "Charlie's ready for you. I really hope the visit goes well. Lucas would make a perfect dad."

Her words hit me in the gut, sending my head spinning, but I quickly pull myself back to reality.

"I hope so too," I agree, returning her smile. "Lucas could really use some company, and I think Charlie might be just what he needs."

"Wait." Chloe throws up a hand. "Lucas is getting a dog?"

"Just a visit, Chloe. Don't get carried away," I say. But I know in my heart how amazing it would be if it grew into more than a visit.

"Right this way," Jayne says, leading us through the maze of kennels to where Charlie eagerly awaits his temporary escape. His soft, dark brown coat and floppy ears make him irresistible, while his wagging tail never stops. Chloe immediately falls for his liquid brown eyes that seem to hold a galaxy of hope, and I have no doubt that he's the perfect companion for Lucas right now.

"Hey there, buddy!" I coo as I approach his cage, and his tail wags even faster. He presses his nose against the bars, sniffing excitedly as if he already knows he's been chosen for a special mission.

"Let's get you out of here, Charlie," Jayne says, unlocking the cage door and clipping a leash onto his collar. Charlie practically leaps out, nearly knocking us over in his enthusiasm, but his excitement is infectious, and I can't help but laugh. Chloe watches us with a grin, her wedding worries momentarily forgotten.

"Be good for Emily and Lucas, okay?" Jayne tells Charlie as she hands me the leash. He looks up at her with those big, soulful eyes and wags his tail as if to promise he'll do his best.

"Thanks, Jayne," I say gratefully. "I owe you one."

"Anything for you and these dogs," she replies, giving me a wink before turning back to her work.

"Alright, let's get going," I announce, leading Charlie and Chloe out of the shelter.

#

With Chloe dropped off at her home in Back Bay, I head toward Lucas's apartment. Her laughter from her interactions with Charlie still echoes in my ears as I drive away, grateful for her understanding and support.

Charlie sits in the back seat, panting happily as he takes in the sights, his nose pressed against the window as if he can't get enough of the world outside. His anticipation is contagious, and I find myself growing more excited by the second.

As we pull up to Lucas's apartment building, I take a deep breath, steadying myself for the moment ahead. Charlie seems to sense my apprehension, nudging my hand with his wet nose and I give him a reassuring pat, as we make our way past the friendly doorman and up the elevator.

I take a deep breath and knock as we enter Lucas's apartment, my heart pounding in anticipation. Charlie wags his tail excitedly, sensing that something wonderful is about to happen.

"In here," Lucas calls out from the living room, his voice low and somber, but welcoming. I step inside, keeping Charlie behind me, as I scan the space, finding him on the mat, winded from a workout. Barely able to contain the grin spreading across my face, I keep Charlie out of view.

"I have a little surprise for you," I say.

Lucas looks up, his weary eyes brightening with curiosity.

"Go get him," I say, laughing as Charlie bounds up to Lucas, his tail wagging furiously. Lucas's eyes widen in surprise and pure joy as he opens his arms for him.

"Hey, boy! Hey, Charlie." His voice cracks with emotion. "How's it going, buddy? It's so good to see you!" Lucas laughs, his face lighting up as he wraps his arms around the dog. They tumble onto the mat together, wrestling playfully. The sight brings tears to my eyes, and I know I've done the right thing.

"Emily, this is amazing," he says, coughing through his constricted throat, his eyes shining. "Thank you."

## Chapter Twenty (Lucas)

Emily was right. Charlie was the exact medicine I needed. And now, as I conquer the fears that threatened to consume me, I do it with them. I do it for them. They're my family now and it's the best thing that's ever happened to me.

I step into the gym, breathing in the familiar scent of sweat and determined preparation that hangs in the air. It's been a few weeks since adopting Charlie and starting work on my PTSD, and I feel proud of the progress I've made. The nightmares have lessened, the panic attacks have gone, and I find myself feeling more at ease when I'm here in my element.

"Hey, Coach!" one of the fighters calls out, waving at me as I make my way over to the mats. "Gimme a roll with Charlie." He takes a solid stance preparing for his pounce.

The other fighters exchange amused glances and it's not long before they're all kneeling on the mats, showering him with attention. I grin at the sight, seeing even my toughest fighters exposing their soft spots.

"Alright, alright," I interrupt their bonding session, clapping my hands together. "Time to get back to work!"

As the group disperses, I lead Charlie over to the side of the room where I can keep an eye on him while I oversee the training exercises. I grab a stopwatch and call out, "Let's start with some grappling drills, everyone! Pair up and get ready!"

Charlie watches intently from the sidelines, sensing the energy in the room. He seems to understand that he's part of the team now, and his eyes follow every movement with interest. It's almost as if he's studying the techniques, eager to learn.

"Come on, guys!" I shout, encouraging them to push themselves harder. "Give it your all!"

Charlie barks in agreement, echoing my sentiment.

The fighters chuckle, and I do too. It feels good to laugh, to let go of the tension that's been building up inside me for so long.

After the practice session, I relax in my office, finalizing plans for our trip to Dubai. We've got a solid team of fighters ready to compete, and my gym's reputation has never been stronger. But it hasn't been without its challenges—securing visas, coordinating travel arrangements, and ensuring our fighters are in peak condition, have all tested my patience and problem-solving skills.

I shake my head, knowing none of it would have been possible without Emily.

The door to my office pushes farther open. "Lucas, you coming back, man?" one of my fighters asks, jolting me out of my thoughts.

"Sure thing," I reply, grabbing my water bottle and heading back toward the mat. We run through some more drills together, each fighter pushing themselves to their limits in preparation for the upcoming tournament.

As we wrap up the session, I glance over at Charlie, who's been watching us intently from the sidelines.

"Alright, that's it for today!" I call out, eliciting groans and sighs. "Rest up, and we'll hit it hard again tomorrow."

As the gym clears out, I leash up Charlie, preparing for a walk to Southie. Emily's been on my mind all day and seeing her is my top priority. With Charlie as my wingman, playing his part as babe-magnet, there's no doubt we'll get her out to walk with us. Although, a small voice in the back of my head keeps nagging me about her recent mood. She's been quiet, standoffish, but I fight the insecurity, knowing it's part of my problem. But no matter my positive self-talk, I can't shake the feeling that something's off.

Charlie and I weave our way through the neighborhoods, his twitching nose attracted to everything, bringing smiles to the most serious of faces. We make our way to Emily's apartment and hit the buzzer. By the time we reach the third floor of her triple-decker, Charlie's tail is wagging a million miles an hour, nearly causing liftoff.

With one scratch on the door, she opens it, and Charlie barrels in, all licks. I pull on his leash. "Hey, boy, that's *my* girl."

Emily lets out a laugh of amusement. "What are you guys doing here?" She runs her fingers through her long hair, trying to control it, but it doesn't matter; she looks beautiful either way.

I glance around her apartment, small but cozy, filled with eclectic furniture and quirky decorations that perfectly reflect her personality. A variety of dog-themed items are scattered throughout the space and

Charlie sniffs at each one. Her laptop is lit up on the coffee table and an empty mug surrounded by old tea bags teeters at the edge.

"We wanted to take you for a walk," I say. "It was Charlie's idea, and I know better than to challenge him."

She gives a weak smile, and it's in that moment that my fears come to the forefront.

"Hey, is everything okay?" I ask, tipping my head to see clearly into her face. She avoids my eyes and moves to the sofa. She sits and slowly closes her laptop.

"Ah, Em?" I ask, sensing the tension in her demeanor.

"Y-yeah, of course," she stammers, avoiding my gaze. "Everything's okay."

It's unlike her to be this reserved around me, which only fuels my concern. Maybe my breakdown was too much for her. I couldn't blame her, I suppose. I *did* fall off the deep end for a moment.

"Emily," I start, looking her straight in the eye. "You know you can talk to me about anything, right?"

She hesitates for a moment before letting out a deep breath. "Yeah, I know, Lucas. It's just... there's something I've been needing to tell you."

My heart drops into my feet and I look for a place to sit. Charlie instinctively stays by my side, offering his support as my life threatens to fall apart in front of me.

"Whatever it is, Em, we'll figure it out together," I assure her, sitting next to her on the couch. She nods, preparing her next words.

My ears are prepared for the inevitable; it's not you it's me, or I had a long talk with Dom, or your PTSD is more than I expected.

I stare at her, allowing her space to speak, as my breath stops in my chest.

She takes a deep breath, looking me in my eyes. "Lucas, I'm... I'm pregnant."

\#

For a moment, the words don't seem to register in my brain, as if they're spoken in a foreign language I can't quite understand. My heart begins to race, and I feel a cold sweat prickling at my brow. My hands tremble as I try to process the information. Is she really...? Are we going to have a baby?

I'm stunned as every emotion in the world attacks me at the same time. Elation. Terror. Love. Panic.

"Did you hear me?" she asks, her voice still trapped in my brain fog.

I clear my throat and shift my position on the couch to face her directly. "Yes," I say. "I'm just, I'm, I'm shocked. When did you find out? How far along are you?"

I hear the fear in my own voice. The thought that she kept this from me for so long was a punch in the gut. Was the baby not mine? Did she not want to keep it? My mind tortures me with toxic scenarios instead of just allowing me to listen to her.

She lowers her gaze from mine. "A couple weeks ago. I'm eight weeks along."

I swallow against the lump in my throat. "Why didn't you tell me sooner?"

"I wanted to. I was just...." She looks away, busying herself with Charlie's collar tags. "I was worried. About how you might react."

"Worried?" My heart begins to race. "Why?"

"Your PTSD." Her voice is gentle. "I didn't want this to trigger an episode. We have so much going on right now, with the Dubai expansion and everything else. I thought if I waited until after—"

"You thought I couldn't handle it." The words come out harsher than I intend, edged with hurt and her eyes jump to mine.

"No, not at all. I just wanted to protect you. To give you time."

"Time for what? To prove I'm not fit to handle something like this?"

"Lucas, stop." She reaches for my hand, and I pull it away. "That's not what this is about at all. I can't do this if you're going to shut me out every time you feel threatened."

Her words hit their mark. I'm overreacting, letting my doubts and insecurities get the better of me.

I sink into the couch, head in my hands. Charlie noses at my knee, offering me comfort. After a moment, I feel Emily's hand on my back, her warmth seeping through my shirt.

I sit up taller and take a deep breath. Everything is okay. Emily is here with me. She isn't leaving. And I realize I can handle this.

"Let's take Charlie for a walk, Em. It might help us clear our heads," I suggest gently, trying to offer her some relief from the tension that seems to have gripped her entire being.

"Okay," she agrees with a small nod, her eyes still downcast.

I leash up Charlie and we head outside, the fresh air feeling like a much-needed reprieve from the stifling atmosphere of the apartment.

As we stroll along the shoreline of Castle Island, the salty ocean breeze brushes our cheeks and chases away the lingering heaviness in the air. Seagulls caw raucously overhead, their cries blending with the gentle lapping of waves against the rocks below. The sun dips lower in the sky, casting a warm glow over the coast.

"Emily, this doesn't change how I feel about you, or us," I say, my voice cracking under the weight of my emotions. "We'll figure it out together."

I guide us towards a nearby bench overlooking the water, feeling as though my legs might give way beneath me at any moment. As we sit down, Charlie hops up onto the seat beside me, his warm, furry body pressed reassuringly against mine. I stroke his fur, trying to ground myself in the present moment.

"Are you okay?" she asks cautiously, her hand finding its way to mine. "I know this is a lot to take in."

"I'm not going to lie, Em, I'm scared," I admit, swallowing the lump in my throat. "I just need to know where your head is at. But please know, I want this. I want you."

"That means the world to me," she replies, tears streaming down her face.

As we sit there, hands clasped and Charlie nestled between us, the weight of Emily's words begins to settle in. My heart rate slows, and the trembling that had taken hold of my body starts to subside. Somehow, despite my initial fear, I feel excitement bubbling up within me as well.

"Em, I need you to know something," I say earnestly, turning to face her. "It may have appeared as terror at first, 'cause it sure felt like it. But now... now it's excitement, hope."

"Really?" she asks, her eyes shining with relief. She smiles through her tears, leaning in to rest her head on my shoulder. "Thank you. For being here, for always being my rock."

"Always," I promise, pressing a gentle kiss to the top of her head. "No matter what."

## Chapter Twenty-One (Emily)

I sit cross-legged on the floor of my apartment, surrounded by an explosion of paper, pens, and half-empty coffee cups. My laptop screen flickers as I try to focus on contract negotiations with the high-end sponsor whose logo will be plastered all over our uniforms. It's a mess in here, and if anyone were to walk in, they'd think a tornado had ripped through the place.

"Okay," I mutter to myself, trying to make sense of the legal jargon swimming across the screen. "Section 4.1... Sponsorship obligations...." My eyes scan back and forth as I attempt to digest the information.

With a sigh, I grab my phone and send Lucas a text message.

*Hey, have you seen these new stipulations from the sponsor? They're asking for a lot. What do you think?*

Minutes tick by, and there's no response. I nibble on my lower lip, hand on my belly, as worry sets in. This isn't like him, he's always been quick to respond, especially when it comes to business matters. I tap out another message.

*Lucas, is everything okay? Haven't heard from you today.*

As I wait for a reply, I glance around the chaos of my apartment—the piles of laundry on the couch, dishes overflowing in the sink, and stacks of dog food bags waiting to be delivered to the shelter. It feels like there aren't enough hours in the day, and with Lucas being unresponsive, my concern only grows.

"Come on, Lucas, where are you?" I mumble under my breath, tapping my fingers against the screen of my phone. A flash of guilt creeps in, making me wonder if I've been too demanding lately with everything going on. My pregnancy caught both of us off guard and I know I have to give us time to fully grasp the idea.

Shaking off the feeling, I send one more text.

*Please let me know what's going on. I'm getting worried.*

My thumb hovers over the Send button for a moment before pressing it.

I stare at my phone, willing it to buzz with a response. As the minutes pass, my mind begins to race with possibilities—is he suffering from a panic attack? Is he having second thoughts about us? Have I pushed him away?

"Damn it, Lucas," I whisper, frustration and worry battling in my chest. "Please just answer me."

As I sit there, surrounded by the chaos of my life, all I can do is hope that whatever is keeping him silent can be resolved. And soon.

The joy of having a little baby inside of me is beyond words. I have to admit when I found out, I immediately considered the scenario of raising him or her by myself. It was wrong of me to jump to the conclusion that Lucas wouldn't want to be involved. I feel guilty about it, but now that he has fallen silent, I'm wondering if my initial thought was correct.

Pacing my cluttered apartment, I know it must be about the pregnancy. Maybe it's triggering his PTSD. I remember how he reacted to the news, knowing it was a tidal wave of emotions.

I know it's a lot for us to face all of a sudden, but in my heart, I believe we can do this. It's not what I had planned for us but having a family with Lucas feels so right. We're meant to do this together, I know it. And I have no doubt he will be an amazing father. I just pray he sees it that way too.

"Enough is enough," I tell myself, grabbing my keys and shoving them into my purse. "I'm going to find out what's going on with him." I make my way down the stairs, determination fueling each step.

The drive is a blur as my emotions take over my rational thought. Reaching the entrance to Lucas's apartment building, my nerves start to get the better of me. What if this just makes things worse? I hesitate in front of the door, but I know I can't live with the uncertainty any longer.

#

I arrive at Lucas's apartment to find him pacing in front of the floor-to-ceiling windows, hands clasped behind his back. He turns at the sound of the door opening, eyes widening briefly before his usual cocky grin slides into place. It doesn't quite reach his eyes. Charlie bounds over to me, tail wagging, and I pet him lovingly behind his ears.

"Em. Wasn't expecting you." His tone is casual, but the tension in his shoulders betrays him.

I cross my arms. "Obviously. Since when do you ignore my texts and calls?"

He winces, scrubbing a hand over the back of his neck. "Yeah, I deserved that. I'm sorry, babe, things have been... complicated."

"How so?" I demand, suspicion flaring as I glance around the open space. There's no sign of another woman, not that I actually believed Lucas would cheat. But his behavior is so out of character, I don't know what else to think. "If this is about the baby, we should—"

"It's not about that," he interrupts, expression softening as he steps forward to take my hands. His are warm and rough, the familiarity instantly soothing my frayed nerves. "The baby is the one good thing I have to look forward to. This is... other stuff. Business complications."

I frown, searching his gaze. Lucas isn't usually this evasive. He's a man who faces problems head-on, as directly and efficiently as he does everything else in life.

"You can tell me," I insist gently. "Whatever it is, we'll deal with it together."

His eyes shutter closed for a brief moment, jaw flexing. When they open again, there's a vulnerability in their depths that I've never seen before. It scares me a little if I'm being honest. Lucas is the strong one, the rock I can depend on. Seeing him like this shakes the foundation of what I've come to believe.

But it also makes me love him more, this glimpse into the parts of himself he usually keeps locked away. I tighten my grip on his hands, willing him to see that he can trust me with anything.

"It's this damn Dubai deal," he admits finally, raking a hand over his hair. "Everything that can go wrong, has."

"What kind of problems?" I ask, not fully believing Dubai is his only worry. "Can they be fixed?"

He huffs out a frustrated breath. "Permit issues, construction delays, partners threatening to pull out unless I fork over more money to keep them happy."

My heart sinks at the distress in his voice. I know how much this means to him, how hard he's worked to put all the pieces in place. Still, there's a hint of relief mingled with my sympathy. At least now I know the radio silence and moodiness of the past weeks had nothing to do with me or the baby. I hope.

I reach up to cup his jaw, offering a comforting smile. "We'll figure something out. If anyone can make this work, it's you." I hesitate for a moment. "Are you sure it's nothing more serious?" I press, unable to shake my lingering skepticism. "You know you can tell me anything, right?"

"Trust me, Emily," he reassures me, his eyes locking on mine. "This is all it is. I promise."

"Okay," I relent, still feeling slightly uneasy. But if Lucas is willing to share this much with me, I'll trust him for now.

"Come on," he says, bumping my shoulder playfully. "Let's make some food. We need to keep you well-fed now at all times."

I smirk as we move into his kitchen.

"I didn't mean to make you worry," he says, pulling out cheese and hummus from the fridge. "I want you to feel safe and secure. It's the only thing that matters now."

I notice the sincerity in his eyes but also see a layer of uncertainty as if his words aren't enough.

I grab a box of crackers and put them on a cutting board. "It's okay. It's all just so new, so many unknowns."

He grins. "Talk about unknowns. Can you imagine us as parents?" He drops the cheese and hummus onto the board and pulls out a knife. "Come on," he says. "Let's bring it out onto the terrace." He gestures towards the sliding glass doors that lead outside.

I grab two waters from the fridge and follow him, feeling the cool evening breeze as we step onto the luxurious rooftop space. He closes the door behind us, leaving Charlie inside. The city lights below us shine like a million fireflies, casting a magical glow over the skyline.

"Wow," I breathe, leaning against the railing and taking in the breathtaking view. "I'll never get tired of seeing this."

I notice the elegant topiary bushes and plush outdoor furniture tucked under a pergola draped with twinkling fairy lights. The space feels intimate and private, offering a sanctuary away from the rest of the world.

"Me neither," Lucas agrees, standing beside me and wrapping an arm around my waist. He leans down to press a tender kiss on my forehead, whispering softly, "Everything is going to be okay, Em. I promise you." He hesitates for a moment. "I know it's just words, but—"

Before he finishes his sentence, he pulls me closer and cradles my face. He leans in and kisses me, warming my insides. All my doubts and fears momentarily vanish, leaving only the comforting certainty that as long as we have each other, we can weather any storm.

"Come here," Lucas murmurs, guiding me over to one of the cushioned chaise lounges. He lowers himself onto the cushions first, then pulls me down to straddle his lap. Our lips meet again, this time with greater hunger, as we lose ourselves in each other's embrace.

His hands roam over my body, expertly untying knots and loosening fabric until I'm down to my bra and panties. The evening air raises goose bumps on my skin, but his touch ignites a fire within me that keeps the chill at bay. Out here in the dark, we're cocooned in our own private world.

"Emily," he groans, his voice thick with desire. "I want you more than anything. All the time."

"Then take me," I reply breathlessly, my eyes locking with his.

Within a single breath, he whips his shirt over his head and pulls off his shorts, somehow keeping a hand on my skin the entire time. His hands roam up my back and he unhooks my bra, exposing my breasts in his face.

He drops his head into my chest, then looks up at me. "You're so beautiful, Emily," he whispers. And I lift his chin and kiss him, pivoting my hips on his lap, causing him to groan. He kisses me deeper, exploring my mouth with his tongue as the heat grows between my legs.

I grind my hips on him instinctively, desperate for him to touch me, as I feel his hardness under my thigh. His hands cup my breasts as his kisses trail down my neck. My head drops back in ecstasy as his mouth finds my nipple and his teeth clamp on it, tugging and sucking.

"Oh my God," I gasp, losing myself to his touch.

He lets out a small laugh and reaches around me, flipping me onto my back on the lounge.

"I'm going to make you beg," he says, moving his kisses down to my belly button.

He slides his thumbs into the sides of my panties and slowly lowers them down my thighs, teasing me with the sensation of lace trailing along my skin.

I hold back, wanting to beg already, the heat within me ready to explode.

And as he moves back up along my thighs, he presses them apart, exposing my wetness to the evening air. He kisses my inner thigh, slowly moving up to my hot folds. And then, his mouth is on me, sliding his tongue over my pink flesh and finding my most sensitive spot. He flicks it with his tongue, tickling it to the point I'm about to scream.

I grab the fabric of the lounge, lifting my hips and spreading my knees to give him full access between my legs. The cool air mixed with his hot breath sends me higher. And then he slides his fingers into me, moving them in and out with precision as he continues to suck me.

"Now, please," I beg.

"Say it," he whispers.

"Fuck me. Please. Fuck me!" I call out.

And in a smooth movement, he's on top of me, positioning his hips between my legs, and he pushes himself into me with a groan.

"Jesus, Emily," he moans, moving in a powerful rhythm that makes me lose my mind.

"Harder," I scream. "Please, Lucas!"

He reaches down, touching my spot as he thrusts inside me, and unable to hold off any longer, I shudder with mind-blowing explosions of passion.

He grunts as he erupts inside me, spasming over me, and then collapses in drained exhaustion.

We pant, holding each other close, smiling with pure satisfaction.

I cling to him, wanting him so badly in my life, wanting him to be my man forever. And all I can do is pray that he'll always want me too.

"You're wonderful," I whisper, still feeling shivers between my legs.

"Everything feels so right with you," he says, gently trailing his fingers over my breast. He takes a deep breath. "There's just one last thing we need to take care of."

I lift my head, looking into his eyes, having no clue what was going through his mind. "What is it?" I ask.

He lets out a slight chuckle. "We need to tell Chloe about our baby."

## Chapter Twenty-Two (Lucas)

I pace back and forth in the gym, my heart thundering in my chest like I'm about to step into the ring for a championship fight. But this isn't any ordinary match—this is the biggest moment of my life. Charlie clings to my heel, following every movement with precision, as if understanding the weight of what's to come. His wagging tail assures me, though, that I'm doing the right thing.

"Lucas, man, you've got this," Xavier says, chuckling as he watches me wear a path into the mats.

"Easy for you to say," I snap, running a hand over my hair. "This is kind of a big deal."

"Oh, I know." He grins. "But you just need to relax and enjoy the moment."

"Relax" and "enjoy" aren't exactly in my vocabulary right now, but I nod, taking a deep breath.

With everything set, I pull out my phone and text Chloe.

*Bring her in.*

"Okay, everyone, places!" I call out to the guys who take their positions around the gym, each wearing their most intimidating game face.

Chloe's response comes almost immediately.

*OMG, I can't believe this is happening!!! On our way.*

"Chloe's bringing her now," I announce, feeling my pulse quicken even more. I glance around the gym, making sure everything is perfect. I straighten the jacket of my gi and tighten the black belt on the uniform.

"Hey, man, remember to breathe," Xavier says, clapping me on the back.

"Thanks," I murmur, focusing on steadying my breaths. I know Emily probably thinks we're just going to tell Chloe about the baby, but I can't wait to see the look on her face when she realizes the real surprise.

"Here goes nothing," I say under my breath as I hear the gym door opening and the sound of Chloe's laughter. This is it—the moment I've been waiting for. My heart is racing, but I'm ready.

My fighters and I stand in formation, all dressed in our formal gis, barefoot. My black gi with my black belt tied around my waist represents both my skill and the importance of this moment. The others wear white gis with their own black belts tied around their waists, creating a powerful contrast that exudes strength and unity.

The gym door opens, and Emily walks in, looking absolutely stunning in her floral dress. The soft fabric hugs her curves, and her long blonde hair flows over her shoulders like a golden waterfall. My heart swells with love and admiration for this incredible woman who has changed my life.

As she looks around the gym, confusion flickers across her face. In my heart, I'm confident this was the best way for me to assure Emily that I am fully committed to her and the baby. She needs to know that I'll always be by her side, no matter what challenges we face together.

"Lucas," she says softly, her eyes searching mine. "What's going on?"

"Emily," I begin, trying to keep my voice steady. "I wanted to do something special for you. You know how much you mean to me, right?"

"Of course," she replies, still confused but smiling now. "But why is everyone all dressed up?" She glances at everyone. "You all look like we're in Dubai already."

"Because today is a very special day," I say, feeling my nerves building as I prepare.

I take a deep breath to calm myself, as I reach out and gently take her hand in mine, feeling the warmth of her skin and the slight tremble at her fingertips.

"Emily," I say, swallowing down the lump in my throat. "You have no idea how much you've changed my life. You saved me from the darkness that was consuming me."

As I speak, I feel my voice choking up with emotion, but I push through it. I need her to understand just how much she means to me. Her eyes widen, and her free hand goes to her mouth as she begins to grasp what's happening.

"Lucas," she whispers, tears welling up in her eyes.

"Emily," I continue, my voice barely audible over the pounding of my heart. "I want to spend the rest of my days loving you, laughing with you, and facing whatever life throws at us, together."

I drop to one knee and pull the ring from the hidden pocket in my gi, holding it up for her to see. The diamond sparkles under the gym's lights, reflecting the excitement I'm feeling. "Emily, will you marry me?"

For a moment, we're both lost in each other's eyes, and I hold my breath, waiting for her answer.

Her breath catches, and tears fill her eyes as they search mine, almost in disbelief. There's no hesitation as she nods, choking out a sob. "Yes, Lucas, I'll marry you."

With trembling hands, I slip the stunning diamond ring onto her finger, relief and joy coursing through me. We're officially engaged, and it feels like the universe has aligned into place.

Chloe, who's been watching along with the fighters, lets out an excited squeal. "Damn, girl! That rock could blind someone!" she exclaims, her eyes wide as she admires the enormous diamond on Emily's finger.

We all laugh, the tension and nerves finally dissipating. I stand up and pull Emily into my arms and kiss her, sealing the moment forever.

The fighters erupt in cheers, their voices resonating through the gym as they clap and holler in celebration. In a show of tradition and camaraderie, they begin to perform a lively tribal dance around Emily and me, their movements swift, agile, and bursting with energy.

"OSS!" they chant in unison, a familiar call that echoes throughout the gym. The sound brings a sense of unity, one that's fitting for the occasion. Their movements are fluid and powerful as they perform the Brazilian dance, circling around us, with Charlie joining in without missing a beat. The synchrony of their steps is mesmerizing, their loyalty to both the sport and to me evident in every motion.

"Oorah! Oorah!" they chant, their voices blending together in a powerful harmony that encapsulates the spirit of jujitsu. I feel a sense of pride swelling within me, knowing that these men—my brothers-in-arms—are here to share in our joy.

Emily's eyes widen in surprise, clearly taken aback by the spectacle. "This is incredible, Lucas," she says, gripping my hand tightly. "I've never seen anything like it."

"It's tradition," I say, grinning broadly.

As the dance continues, Chloe sneaks away and reappears moments later with her arms laden with champagne bottles and glasses.

"Let's make this official, shall we?" she asks, winking at us as she hands each of us a flute. As I pop the cork on the first bottle, the sound echoes through the gym, eliciting another round of cheers from the fighters, and I fill the glasses.

"Here's to Emily and Lucas," Chloe announces, raising her glass in a toast. "May your love be strong, everlasting, and filled with laughter!"

"Cheers!" We all reply in unison, clinking our glasses together. As I take a sip of the champagne, I notice Emily merely pretends to drink, subtly bringing the glass to her lips without actually swallowing any of it. I know she's trying to keep her pregnancy a secret for now.

She steps closer to Chloe. "So, you knew about this?" she accuses her with a hip bump.

"Guilty as charged," she says. "And believe me, helping to choose the ring was quite the experience. I know how particular you can be," she teases.

"Hey!" Emily protests playfully, her eyes sparkling with amusement.

"Anyway," Chloe continues, "We finally found the perfect one after visiting what felt like a million jewelry stores. The moment Lucas saw it, he just knew it was the one."

Emily nods with a smile and glances at me. Her head tips like she's trying to figure something out. She sneaks closer to me.

"Wait," she whispers, furrowing her brow. "Is this why you've been so quiet these past few days?"

"I didn't mean to come across that way, but yes," I say, wrapping my arm around her waist protectively. "I was just trying to keep everything a secret. I wanted this to be the perfect surprise for you."

"Mission accomplished," she replies, planting a tender kiss on my cheek.

"Besides," I confess with a sheepish grin, "I might have been a little nervous about getting everything just right. I mean, it's not every day you propose to the love of your life."

"Wait until we start planning the wedding," Chloe teases, winking at Emily. "That's when the real fun begins!"

She chuckles, squeezing my hand nervously.

I lean down to her ear. "We're going to have to tell her about the baby."

She swallows hard. "That's exactly what I was just thinking."

I squeeze her hand back. "No better time than the present?" My brows lift as I seek her agreement.

"Emily, let me top you up!" Chloe exclaims, reaching for the champagne bottle with a grin. She pauses mid-pour, her eyes darting between Emily's untouched champagne and the knowing look that passes between us. Her brow furrows with suspicion, and I can practically see the gears turning in her head.

"Okay, what's going on here?" Chloe demands, crossing her arms over her chest.

I glance at Emily again and she nods her approval.

"So, uh, Chloe," I start. "There's a second part to all of this."

Her eyes dart between Emily and me.

And before I can say another word, she drops her head back with a huge groan.

"That's not fair," she bellows. "Emily! You beat me to it!" She reaches her arms around her and gives her a warm hug. "Oh my God, you two are going to make amazing parents."

Emily laughs, and I watch as Chloe's surprise and joy shift to a larger realization.

"Wait," she grumbles. Her face falls from the unexpected change to her planner. "Does this mean you'll be getting married before me too?"

## Chapter Twenty-Three
## (Emily)

The cardboard boxes surrounding me seem to have multiplied since I started packing this morning. Focusing on the task at hand, I fold another box and tape it shut, and take a quick glance at my beautiful diamond. I can't believe all of this is happening, a baby, an engagement, a trip to Dubai. I'm overjoyed with how things have been going. It makes it all the easier to release my freelance clients and put my entire focus on the growing Walker Enterprises.

"Emily, did you pack the extra rash guards?" Lucas calls out from across the gym, his voice steady and confident, Charlie trailing behind him like a second shadow, as always.

"Yep, got 'em," I reply, checking off the items on my mental list. With each completed task, I feel more prepared for what lies ahead in Dubai. Preparing a team for a world championship has been quite an undertaking and, in all honesty, I'm feeling the competitive thrill in my bones.

Lucas approaches me, a grin plastered on his face. "I have to say, our fighters have never been more ready for such a showcase. You'll be amazed to see them in full competition mode."

"You guys deserve it all," I tell him.

"Absolutely," he says with a wink. "You know what they say: keep your eyes solidly on your goals, and you'll always win." He leans against the wall, crossing his arms over his chest. "I'm really proud of everyone here. They're dedicated, talented, and more than willing to put in the hard work. I couldn't ask for a better group to represent us in Dubai."

I nod, realizing I've never been exposed to this kind of thing before—a sport that pulls the fighters together like a brotherhood, each one giving their heart and soul to it. I pick up a box and push open the door, feeling grateful to be a part of something so real.

With the sun beating down on us, we load the last of the boxes into Lucas's SUV, while Charlie perches protectively by his side.

"Is that everything?" I ask, wiping my brow with the back of my hand.

"Looks like it," he says, taking a moment to survey our work. "Let's get these bad boys to the airport storage unit."

As we're about to close the tailgate, Charlie's ears perk up and he starts barking and growling, drawing our attention to a blacked-out sedan pulling into the parking lot. My breath catches in my throat when I recognize the driver—Carlo. My first instinct is to worry that Lucas will lose his cool with him again, but as I glance over at him, I know he'll manage the situation just fine.

"Carlo," he murmurs, his voice cold and unyielding, as he takes a defensive stance in front of me. He holds his gaze on the car, anticipating what's to come.

I hold my breath, waiting for the confrontation I'm sure is about to ensue, but instead of getting out of the car, Carlo rolls down his window, his eyes never leaving Lucas's.

"Hey man, listen. I need to talk to you," Carlo begins, and I can almost see the wheels turning in Lucas's mind as he tries to figure out what game Carlo is playing this time. "I've got a problem, and I could use your help."

"Really?" Lucas scoffs, crossing his arms over his chest. "This should be interesting."

"Look, I know we've had our differences," Carlo admits, finally glancing in my direction before quickly averting his gaze. "But this isn't about me. It's about my fighters. They've been training hard, and they deserve a shot at the championship."

"As do mine. Get to the point," Lucas snaps, his patience wearing thin.

"Alright," Carlo sighs. "My gym's been excluded from the Dubai tournament." Lucas's eyes grow wide. "False accusations, but I don't have time to get into the details. I'm asking if you'll take my top fighters with you—let them compete as part of the Walker Enterprises team. They deserve a chance, man."

The silence that follows is heavy with tension, as Lucas weighs his options. It would be so easy for him to turn Carlo down, to refuse to help the man who's caused us so much grief. But then I see the resolve in his eyes, and I know he'll make the right decision—not just for him, but for the sport he loves.

"Fine," he finally says, taking a step closer to Carlo, his voice steady and strong. "We'll take your fighters. And maybe this will be a lesson to you, to follow the right path, for the honor of the sport." He stares Carlo down, holding his position.

"Understood," he replies, swallowing hard as he meets Lucas's unwavering gaze. Then he opens the car door and gets out. He reaches for

Lucas's hand, and I can tell by the look on his face that he respects him.

Lucas nods, accepting Carlo's handshake. "We'll take good care of your fighters. And when we win that championship, they'll get their share of the prize money and prestige. Fair is fair."

"You're a good man, Walker," Carlo says, patting his shoulder as he nods in gratitude. "Thank you. You won't regret this. They're good guys. Good fighters."

"Like I said, fair is fair. May the best fighters win." Lucas releases his grip, turning to the open door of the SUV. Carlo nods at me, arms by his sides, then climbs into his sedan and pulls out of the parking lot with a crunch of gravel.

Lucas goes to close the tailgate, but I catch his arm, halting his movements. "That was really big of you."

He shakes his head as if it were nothing. "He's still a jackass, but his fighters don't deserve to suffer because of it." He shrugs. "And who knows? Maybe this will be a turning point for Carlo. Help him clean up his act. There's no need for the local dojos to fight against each other."

I wrap my arms around him, overcome with emotion for the man he is and what he stands for. I beam up at him, filled with warmth and affection. He's always had a strong sense of justice, but to see him put it into action, even when it means helping a rival. It only makes me love him more.

It makes me realize that this is the life I always hoped for—standing beside a partner whose strength and integrity match my own, ready to face any challenge that comes our way.

"I love you," I whisper into his ear, and he lifts me up, swinging me around in his strong arms.

"I love you too, babe," he says, setting me down gently. "And you know what I've been thinking?"

I look at him, eyebrows lifted.

And he continues, "I'm thinking we should get married while we're in Dubai."

#

As I watch Carlo's car move out of sight, I turn back to Lucas, my heart swelling with pride. He's made a difficult decision, one that could have easily turned sour, but he chose fairness and compassion over personal grudges. And now he's turning the decision into something positive, talking about our wedding.

"Lucas," I breathe, my eyes shining with admiration. "You never cease to amaze me. Your strength, your integrity... I'm so proud of you, and I know helping Carlo will only make Walker Enterprises stronger."

He smiles, as he pulls me into his embrace. "It's all because of you, Em," he says softly. "You inspire me to be better every day."

I reach up and kiss him, loving the warmth of his mouth on mine, his breath on my face.

He deepens the kiss, one hand sliding into my hair to angle my head. I melt against him, heat building in me as giddy joy swirls in my chest. When we break apart, we're both a little breathless.

"I love you," I say softly, still close enough that my lips brush his with every word. "So much."

He smiles down at me, blue eyes glinting. "I love you too." He ducks his head, nuzzling his nose into my neck. "You've made me the luckiest man on earth."

"Funny," I murmur. "I was just thinking the same thing."

His laughter is warm and rough, vibrating against my skin. "Then it seems we were made for each other, Mrs. Walker." He pulls back and looks at me. "I can see it now. A beach wedding at sunset, surrounded by a team of jujitsu warriors." His eyes sparkle with mischief. "What do you say? Want to get married in paradise?"

My breath catches at the image he paints. A private wedding on the beach, pledging myself to him under the golden light of a setting sun in Dubai. It's perfect. Romantic and dramatic, just like Lucas. Just like us.

I blink in surprise, then let out a burst of laughter. "Really? Just like that?"

"Hey, why not?" he shrugs, still grinning. "We've already got the backdrop for some epic wedding photos, and we can start our lives together as husband and wife right away. Plus, it'll be one hell of a story to tell our grandkids someday."

"Getting married in a foreign country while overseeing an international jujitsu championship?" I muse, my mind racing at the thought.

"Exactly!" he agrees, his enthusiasm infectious. "Besides, do you really want to wait any longer? What's the point, Mrs. Walker?"

"Mrs. Walker, huh?" I say, testing the name on my tongue. "I have to admit, it does have a nice ring to it."

"See? It's perfect," he insists, wrapping his arms around me again. "So, Emily, will you marry me in Dubai?"

"If you're completely serious, Mr. Walker," I say softly. "Then the answer is yes. A thousand times yes."

His arms tighten around me, crushing me close against his hard chest. I feel the acceleration of his heart under my palm, the warmth of his breath against my hair. "Completely serious," he whispers.

I laugh, blinking back the sting of tears. "It sounds perfect."

He pulls back to look down at me, eyes shining with emotion. "Well, sounds like we've got some extra planning to do, and very little time to do it. But I'll make it happen, no matter what." He dips his head again, sealing his promise with a deep, claiming kiss.

When we finally break apart, I'm breathless for an entirely different reason. "So," I say lightly, "Now we're going to be in ever bigger trouble with Chloe."

He laughs. "It's perfect. She was too self-consumed by her own wedding anyway." He shakes his head with a huff. "Maybe she'll see it's not about her all the time."

"You really think so?" I chuckle.

"Nope. But one can dream."

# Chapter Twenty-Four
## (Lucas)

I watch as my fighters gather at the gym for our final ceremony before leaving for the Dubai showcase. Their excitement and anticipation fill the air, and I feel a surge of pride for what we've built together. My gaze drifts to Emily, standing near the edge of the group, looking gorgeous in the new white gi I bought her. The white belt tied around her waist highlights her slender figure, and I know she's trying her best to blend in, though I can see the uncertainty in her eyes.

"Alright, everyone! Let's begin!" I call out, and the room quiets down. We form a circle, hands on each other's shoulders, feeling the strength in our unity. This Brazilian Jujitsu ceremony is an essential part of our tradition, invoking good luck, health, and wellness for the upcoming battles.

The music begins, a rhythmic beat that echoes through the space, and one of Carlo's fighters starts pounding on a drum, adding depth to the sound. The team unifies as one through the music and traditional ritual, and I think about how far we've come since our rivalry with Carlo began. Despite his underhanded tactics, we've stayed true to our morals, and it shows in the solidarity among us.

As the chanting starts, the energy in the room shifts, lifting higher with each syllable. The words are ancient, passed down through generations of fighters, and they carry the weight of our collective dreams and aspirations. I join in, letting the sounds pour from my soul, feeling the power it brings.

"Lucas," Emily whispers, leaning into me, "I don't know the words."

I chuckle quietly, not wanting to break the spell. "Just hum along. It's more about the feeling than the lyrics."

She nods, closing her eyes for a moment as she finds the rhythm, her body swaying ever so slightly. I smile at her determination to be a part of this, to support me and my team in every way possible.

As the ceremony continues, I feel a growing sense of gratitude for the family we have created here. We're more than just a group of fighters; we're a tribe, bound together by our passion and dedication. And with Emily by my side, I know that nothing can stand in our way.

"Here's to victory in Dubai!" I raise my voice over the music, and the room erupts into cheers and applause.

"Victory!" they echo, their spirits soaring high, ready to take on the world.

"Who's first?" I call out, the chant fading away as each fighter prepares to take a turn in the center of the circle.

My head nods with pride as my team members demonstrate their techniques, some slick and smooth, others powerful and intense. I see years of dedication and hard work in every move they make, and it fills me with confidence for what lies ahead.

"Go, Daniel!" Emily shouts enthusiastically, clapping her hands together as he executes an impressive armbar. I chuckle at her enthusiasm, knowing she's still learning the techniques, but her support is contagious.

"Nice move, man!" I add, slapping Daniel on the back as he returns to the circle's edge.

As each fighter showcases their skills, the energy in the room intensifies. They feed off each other's determination, and I feel the fire burning within them, ready to take on anyone who stands between us and victory in Dubai.

"Your turn, Lucas," Xavier nudges me, his eyes sparkling with excitement. I nod, stepping into the center of the circle.

With a deep breath, I unleash a series of moves, demonstrating the fluidity and power that has carried me through countless battles. Cheers erupt around me, and I smile, knowing that my team has my back.

Emily watches me intently, her eyes wide. I sense her belief in me, and it fuels my every movement.

"Amazing, Lucas!" she exclaims as I finish my demonstration. It's impossible not to laugh at her enthusiasm, and I pull her into a tight hug.

"Thanks, babe," I murmur into her ear, feeling the warmth of her body pressed against mine.

As the ceremony progresses, our focus sharpens, and our determination grows. We're not just here for ourselves; we're here for each other, for the tribe we've built together.

"Remember, guys," I say as the last fighter finishes their demonstration, my voice steady and strong, "we're in this together. No matter what happens in Dubai, we have each other's backs."

They respond with tribal calls and backslaps.

"Emily," Xavier calls out, gesturing for her to join us in the circle. As she hesitates, I reach out and give her hand a reassuring squeeze.

"Go on, Em. You've got this," I encourage her, my voice low and steady.

"Alright," she sighs, stepping into the circle, her white gi contrasting with her flushed cheeks. The fighters begin to chant and dance around her, their voices resonating throughout the gym.

At first, Emily appears uncomfortable, shifting her weight from one foot to the other as if she's unsure of what to do. But then, the rhythm of the drum seems to reach her, and she starts swaying to the beat, her movements growing more confident with each passing moment.

"Come on, Emily!" one of the fighters shouts encouragingly, and soon they're all cheering for her.

"Você consegue, garota" another one adds, his voice full of admiration. She doesn't understand Portuguese, but the tone is enough for her to know that it's good.

Seeing Emily, so completely embraced by the team, her hair flying around her as she moves like some sort of goddess, fills me with an indescribable sense of pride.

"Lucas, look at your girl!" Xavier exclaims, clapping me on the back. "She feels it!"

"Damn right, she does," I reply, unable to tear my eyes away from her. In this moment, with the drums beating and the chanting filling the air, I see Emily as a true part of our tribe.

"Em, você é incrível!" I shout over the noise, wanting her to know just how much this means to me.

Her eyes shine with excitement and joy.

As the ceremony continues and the energy in the room grows even more intense, I think about the incredible journey Emily and I have shared together. From our initial attraction to our stubborn clashes over business to our unwavering love for one another, we've faced it all—and come out stronger for it.

"Alright, everyone!" Xavier calls out as the ceremony comes to a close. "Let's give it up one more time for the tribe!"

The fighters chant their final calls, their voices filling the gym with strength and unity.

"Vamos lá, equipe!" I shout, raising my fist in the air. "We're going to bring home the gold!"

"Sim!" they echo, their voices filled with determination.

Just as my heart starts to slow down from the thrill of watching Emily embrace our team's traditions, Xavier gives me a playful shove into the circle with her. The chants grow louder and more intense, their rhythm pulsing through my veins as I join Emily in the center.

"The happy couple," Xavier grins, his eyes sparkling with mischief. "Show us what you've got!"

Emily looks at me hesitantly, her cheeks flushed from dancing, but I give her a reassuring nod. It's time for us to show ourselves as a couple and as members of this team.

"Ready?" I ask, my voice barely audible over the pounding drums and chanting fighters.

"Ready," she replies with a determined smile, her eyes locking on mine.

We start to move in slow circles together, our bodies mirroring each other's movements as we perform a series of slow-motion jujitsu moves. I feel the energy in the room intensify, our connection evident to everyone present. As we finish, I pull her into a tight embrace and dip her back, our lips meeting in a passionate kiss that sets the gym ablaze with cheers.

"Go Coach!" one of the fighters hollers, clapping and laughing as we break apart, breathless and grinning.

"Alright, team!" I call out, raising my hands to quiet the room. "Let's get ready for Dubai!"

The chants begin to fade, replaced by heartfelt affirmations and wishes for success in the upcoming tournament. As we gather in a tight circle, arms around each other, the strength of our camaraderie courses through me.

"Remember," I tell them, my voice steady and confident, "we are stronger together than any one of us could ever be alone. Trust in your training, trust in your teammates, and trust in yourselves. We're going to win this thing!"

"Vamos lá!" they echo.

\#

As the gym empties out and the energy from the ceremony lingers, I pause for a moment to truly take in just how far we've all come. It's a feeling like no other, knowing that this group of fighters has become more than just teammates; they're family, bound by our shared love and passion for jujitsu.

"Can you believe it?" Emily murmurs, gazing around the room. "Not too long ago, I would have never imagined being part of something so incredible."

"Neither would I," I confess, pulling her into my embrace. "But look at us now. I wouldn't trade it for anything in the world."

As if on cue, the door to the gym swings open and Chloe strides inside, her arms laden with a tray of homemade cupcakes. "Alright, you two," she sings, grinning mischievously. "It's time for some pre-tournament sugar!"

"Chloe!" Emily exclaims, disentangling herself from me and rushing over. "I was hoping you'd come!"

"Did I miss anything?" she asks, setting the tray down on a nearby table, clueless to the launch ceremony that just went down. "I'm not letting my favorite people fly off to Dubai without a proper send-off."

Emily glances at me with a smirk.

"Speaking of Dubai," I say, exchanging a nod with Emily before turning back to Chloe. "We actually have something we need to tell you."

"Something important," Emily adds, her voice slightly shaky.

Chloe's eyes narrow in suspicion as she looks back and forth between us. "Alright, spill it. What's going on?"

"Chloe, we...," I start, taking a deep breath before continuing. "we've decided to get married while we're in Dubai."

"Dubai?" she gasps, her eyes widening in shock. "Like, now?"

"Surprise," Emily offers weakly.

"Wow," she breathes, clearly taken aback. "I mean, that's awesome! I'm just a little shocked."

"We wanted to do something special, something that truly symbolizes our journey together," I explain, as I wrap an arm around Emily's waist. "And since we're going to be there anyway, it just felt like the perfect opportunity."

Chloe's shoulders sink slightly, absorbing the sudden plans. "I, I just always thought I'd be a part of both of your weddings," she murmurs. "But I understand."

Emily steps forward, holding out a neatly folded white gi adorned with a bouquet of flowers, a plane ticket peeking out from beneath the fabric. "We have a little surprise for you."

Chloe looks up and sees the gi, confusion on her face. "You want me to learn jujitsu too?" she asks.

Emily laughs, looking down at her own gi. "No, Chloe. We want you to come with us." And she tugs the plane ticket out and hands it to her. As Chloe sees her name on the ticket, her eyes light up and mist over. "Will you be my maid of honor?"

I step closer and put my arm around her shoulder. "We'd both be honored to have you there to represent us."

For a moment, it's as if time stands still, the air thick with anticipation. Chloe stares at us, her jaw slack, her eyes wide.

"Is this... is this for real?" she finally manages to ask, her voice wavering.

"Absolutely," I confirm, feeling a warmth spreading through my chest as I watch Chloe struggle to process the news.

"Wow." Chloe blinks rapidly, tears pooling in her eyes. "I mean, I never expected Emily to get married before me, but... wow."

"I didn't plan it this way, I swear," Emily jokes lightly, trying to break the tension.

"Clearly." Chloe lets out a shaky laugh and then, taking a deep breath, she looks at us both, determination shining in her eyes. "I would be absolutely honored to be your maid of honor."

As we stand there, the three of us wrapped up in each other's arms, I realize that this is what true happiness feels like. We're a family, and we have our tribe, and I couldn't be happier.

# Chapter Twenty-Five (Emily)

The airport terminal buzzes with energy and anticipation as I walk hand-in-hand with Lucas. My heart races, and I can't help but smile, thinking about the adventure that awaits us. Dubai, a city of luxury and extravagance—is the perfect backdrop for Lucas's jujitsu team to compete in the international tournament.

"Are you excited?" he asks, squeezing my hand gently.

"Excited" doesn't even begin to cover it. This trip represents so much: our future together, the success of his business, and our hard work and determination. I nod enthusiastically, unable to find words to express my emotions.

As we round a corner in the bustling terminal, we spot them, the Walker Enterprises team, decked out in sleek black tracksuits and hoodies emblazoned with the team logo. The bright orange pouncing tiger can be seen on each piece of merchandise, its claws extending out, reaching for victory. The team huddles together, exuding an air of camaraderie and confidence that makes me grin from ear to ear.

"Lucas! Emily!" Xavier calls out, his voice booming through the terminal. He strides toward us, arms open wide, and pulls us into a fierce group hug. "I can't believe it's finally here."

"Xavier," Lucas says, clapping him on the back, "there's no better fighter, no better man to have as my best man." The sincerity in his voice is palpable, and I see the pride in Xavier's eyes as he grins at his friend.

"Thanks, man. You know I've got your back, always," he replies, his loyalty evident in every word.

As the team converges around us, exchanging high fives and good-natured teasing, I take a moment to absorb the scene before me. These are the people who have become like family, and I couldn't be more grateful for their unwavering support of both Lucas and me.

"Alright, team!" Lucas exclaims, drawing everyone's attention. "We've got a flight to catch and a tournament to win. Let's do this!"

A chorus of cheers echoes through the terminal as we prepare for our journey to Dubai, hearts full of excitement and anticipation. And as I glance at Lucas, his eyes shining with determination, I know that together, we are unstoppable.

"Can you believe we're actually going to Dubai?" Chloe squeals, bouncing up and down on her toes as she clutches my arm. "This is going to be amazing!"

"I know!" I exclaim, sharing in her enthusiasm. "I've never been that far from home before, and it's all so exciting." I paused for a second. "Hey, was your mom good with taking Charlie while we're gone?"

"Oh, yes, trust me. She's going to spoil him rotten." She laughs. "And now, you get to see Lucas kick some serious butt," she adds with a wink.

"I know," I reply, grinning at the thought of Lucas in the tournament. It's true; his focus and determination are part of what makes him so attractive to me. But right now, he's all business, discussing strategy with Xavier and the rest of the team. He's completely in his element, and I can't help but admire him from afar.

"Em," he calls out suddenly, motioning for me to join him. I give Chloe a quick wave and head over to where he's standing, feeling a flutter of anticipation in my stomach.

"Hey," he says softly, pulling me aside so we're out of earshot of the others. "I don't want to miss a moment of this with you. I just wanted to tell you... I can't wait for you to be my wife."

"Really?" I ask, touched by his words. "Even with all the chaos of the tournament?"

"Especially because of the chaos," he admits, smiling warmly at me. "You're the calm in the storm, Emily. You ground me, remind me of what's important. And I can't imagine facing any challenge, on or off the mat, without you by my side."

"Lucas," I whisper, tears pricking at the corners of my eyes. "I can't wait to be your wife."

"Good," he replies, brushing a stray tear from my cheek. "Because I mean every word. And when we return from Dubai, we'll start our incredible life together." He puts his hand on my belly. "As a family."

"Sounds perfect," I agree, beaming up at him.

"Speaking of," Lucas says, his eyes twinkling with mischief, "have you given any thought to where you want to live after we're married? I suppose that's the next thing to think about when we get back."

"Um, not really," I admit, a little taken aback by the question. "I guess I just assumed we'd live in your place." I hesitate for a moment. "Or mine," I mumble, suddenly feeling insecure about my tiny apartment compared to his luxurious penthouse.

"Both are great options," he reassures me, squeezing my hand gently. "But I was thinking that maybe we could go house hunting when we get back from Dubai. Find a place that's truly ours, you know? Anywhere you want."

"Wow." My eyes widen at the suggestion, excitement bubbling inside me. "That sounds amazing!" I didn't think my excitement could go any higher, but the thought of returning from this trip to an adventure of finding a house is beyond thrilling.

"Great!" Lucas grins, clearly pleased with my reaction. "We'll make a plan as soon as we're home."

"Did someone say 'home'?" Chloe suddenly pops up beside us, her eyes gleaming with curiosity. "Are you two talking about where you're going to live after the wedding?"

"Uh, yeah," I confirm, shooting Lucas an amused glance. "We were just discussing the idea of finding a new place together."

"Ooh! You should totally move onto my street!" she exclaims, clapping her hands in delight. "There's this gorgeous house for sale just a few doors down from me, and it would be so fun to be neighbors!"

"Neighbors?" I chuckle at her enthusiasm. Turning to Lucas, I raise an eyebrow, silently asking for his opinion on the matter.

"Sounds like it could be fun," he concedes, beaming at Chloe. "We'll definitely look into it."

"Yay!" Chloe squeals, bouncing on her toes with excitement. "Just imagine all the impromptu barbecues and game nights we could have!"

"Chloe, your excitement is contagious," I laugh, feeling my enthusiasm grow at the thought of living so close to my best friend.

"See? It's meant to be!" she declares, nodding her head with conviction. "I can't wait to help you guys move in and decorate your new love nest."

As we join the rest of our team, preparing to board our flight to Dubai, I feel a sense of exhilaration. Everything is falling into place and a true feeling of joy fills me.

With Chloe's excitement still fresh in the air, Lucas gently takes my hand and leads me a few steps away from the group. His eyes hold a hint of amusement as he leans down to whisper in my ear, "As much as I adore Chloe and her boundless energy, I'm not sure living on the same street is the best idea for us."

"Oh, thank God," I say with a huge exhale. "And here I thought you were thrilled at the prospect of impromptu barbecues and game nights."

"Thrilled might be an overstatement," he replies, his lips curling into a smirk. "I do love Chloe, but a little distance might keep our sanity intact."

"I couldn't agree more," I concede, chuckling softly. As much as I love Chloe, Lucas and I need space to build our own lives. But I'll be sure her feelings don't get hurt in the process.

*"Attention passengers, this is the final boarding call for flight EK222 to Dubai, departing from gate B7,"* the airport PA system announces, jolting us back to the present moment.

"Looks like it's time to go," I say, squeezing Lucas's hand. He nods, his eyes filled with excitement as we make our way back to our team.

"Alright, everyone, let's get moving! Dubai awaits!" Lucas calls out, his authoritative tone effortlessly commanding their attention.

"Did someone say Dubai?" Xavier chimes in with a grin.

"Everyone, circle up!" Lucas announces as we stand near our gate. The Walker Enterprises team forms a tight cluster, arms around each other's shoulders, their excitement bubbling over.

"Alright, guys, this is it," Lucas says, his eyes sparkling with determination. "We've trained hard for this tournament, and I know we're going to crush it!"

"Damn right, we are!" Xavier exclaims along with the others.

"Okay, guys," Lucas says, drawing our attention back to him. "One last time before we board—let's hear our fight chant!"

Xavier stands tall, preparing to lead the chant.

Everyone in the huddle begins to bounce as they follow his rhythm. "Jujitsu! Forte e Verdadeiro! A vitória está à vista, essa é a nossa visão!"

They repeat the victory chant three times, growing louder with each verse, sending chills through me. As we bounce and shout, the energy in our circle crackles like a live wire, electrifying every inch of my body. Other passengers watch us with a mix of awe and amusement, clearly impressed.

"Alright, team," Lucas says once the chant ends, his voice filled with pride. "Let's go kick some ass in Dubai!"

"Kick-ass" seems to be the theme of our lives lately—both in and out of the gym. From overcoming personal obstacles to building a loving, supportive relationship, Lucas and I have proven that we can conquer anything life throws our way.

And as we near the plane, arm in arm, I know that no matter what happens in Dubai—or anywhere else for that matter—we'll face it head-on, side by side, with all the passion that brought us together in the first place.

As our tribe moves toward the plane, the anticipation in the air is palpable. This trip marks the beginning of a new chapter for all of us—not just Lucas and me, but for the entire Walker Enterprises team.

"Last call for flight to Dubai," the announcement blares over the airport speakers, adding urgency to our steps. We exchange excited looks, knowing that our great adventure is about to begin.

"Looks like we made it," Lucas says, guiding me toward the open plane door. His warm fingers brush against my wrist, sending shivers up my spine despite the bustle around us.

As we board the plane and settle into our seats, a sense of satisfaction washes over me. We've come so far, both individually and as a couple, and the future stretches out before us like an endless horizon, filled with possibility and promise.

"Hey," Lucas whispers, leaning in close and brushing a stray strand of hair from my face. "You ready for this?"

"Absolutely," I reply, catching his hand and giving it a reassuring squeeze. "Together, we're unstoppable."

"Damn right we are," he says, his voice warm and full of conviction.

Arm in arm, we watch the runway disappear beneath us as the plane lifts off, soaring toward our next big adventure.

# Special Offer

If you enjoyed this book, then you will love **_"Falling For the Forbidden Billionaire"_** It's FREE on Kindle Unlimited and you can get it here.

★★★★★ "This book has so much Drama. You'll put it down thinking if it weren't for bad luck, Eden wouldn't have any luck at all. You'll laugh, you'll cringe and you'll SQUEEEEE like a teenage girl. This book is very well written and will have you wanting to finish it in one sitting." – Reader review

**A chaotic wedding reception jeopardizes my best friend Tori's event-planning business. Her hot billionaire brother swoops in, saves me, and restores order.** His stunning good looks and charm leave me breathless. But he is off-limits as my bestie's brother. Despite that, he hires me as his personal assistant when I lose my job. We can't resist each other, and a passionate one-night stand follows. But powerful men have powerful enemies. Unaware, my life will soon be in danger at the hands of his fiercest rival. Oh, and I'm pregnant.

You can start reading it right here.

Manufactured by Amazon.ca
Bolton, ON